Canyon Lake

Melanie Gaines

Canyon Lake

Published by Wheatmark™
610 East Delano Street, Suite 104, Tucson, Arizona 85705 U.S.A.
www.wheatmark.com

Cover Photo – Courtesy of Wayne Heupel
Author Photo – Courtesy of Dwight Gaines

Publisher's Cataloging-In-Publication Data
(Prepared by The Donohue Group, Inc.)

Gaines, Melanie.
  Canyon Lake / Melanie Gaines.

  p. ; cm.

  ISBN-10: 1-58736-671-1
  ISBN-13: 978-1-58736-671-0

1. Canyon Lake (Ariz.)--Fiction. 2. Lifesaving--Fiction. 3. Landscape painting--Fiction. 4. Deserts--Arizona-- Fiction. 5. Romantic suspense fiction. I. Title.

PS3607.A36 C36 2006
813./6   2006928986

This book is lovingly dedicated to the next
generation of
swimmers, artists,
musicians, and athletes
who can do it all.

James, Cynthia, and Daniel

". . . infinite passion and the pain
of finite hearts that yearn."
Robert Browning

ACKNOWLEDGMENTS

WHILE THE CHARACTERS IN this book are fictional, many of the incidents occurred. The author wishes to thank a number of people who have helped greatly in the evolution of this book and its production.

The team at Wheatmark Publishing; especially my editor, Lori Sellstrom.

Charles Ferguson of the Arizona Geological Survey in Tucson who provided me with his expert knowledge of the land formations in and around Canyon Lake.

Robin Miller and his music, "In the company of ANGELS" that was able to summon my writing muse when nothing else would.

To all my proofreaders, who shared with me their valuable insights.

Dwight, my husband, saying "thank you" is not enough for your editing and consulting. Your encouragement has kept me going. I could not have done this without you.

To all my family and friends who knew I was struggling, and continued to give me the needed boost of encouragement when I needed it.

My parents, Monty and Yvonne Fox, who still avoid the water, but through their boundless love, keep our family afloat.

My sisters, Kathy and Tracy, and brother, Monty, and their families, for their enduring love and support.

A special thanks to the artist who started the ball rolling, Jo Watts-Sullivan, for her beautiful painting of Canyon Lake, which has occupied a prominent place in my home since that July stroll through the gallery.

And especially to those past who will not be forgotten; John and Dorothy Fox, Ray and Anita Sage, and Uncle John. Your spirits live in my heart forever.

AUTHOR'S NOTE

THE NEAR-DROWNING EVENT IN this story really did happen. The painting is real, but the artist in this story is a fictitious character created from the author's own imagination. This unfolding story is one version of how these events could have ended.

The author's family never found out who the man was that saved her parents. Because he disappeared so quickly after her parents were pulled from the water, they came to think of him as an angel, sent to them at that exact moment, at that exact place, to change the course of their lives. They will never know who he was, but they will be forever grateful that there are angels among us.

1

~ *Rae* ~

The Dream

I woke up in a twist of bed sheets, and my body felt slick with morning sweat. The skin between my legs and under my breasts felt wet and sticky as if I hadn't bathed in a week. I laid there, wide-eyed and panic-stricken, trying to focus my eyes and restore my breathing to normal. I looked around the dim, early morning lit room and realized, from my own mussed bed, that the house remained quiet. I swung my legs out of the damp sheets and sat up against the cool metal bars of my headboard.

Not the dream again, I said to myself as I pushed my tangled, long hair from my face. I thought by now the nightmares were gone for good. After all, I found what I had been looking for all these years. *Damn,* I thought, as I slid to the edge of the bed and put my feet on the cool, wood floor. I reached to my bedside table for the wooden pick to coil up my hair with, away from my neck, as the perspiration continued to bead up on my skin. A slight smile came to my lips at the sight of the half-eaten apple leaning against a stale glass of water left over from the night before. I looked over my shoulder at the still sleeping form of the man I now shared my bed with. I leaned over gently to put my face against his to smell his warm morning scent of our shared passions from the night before. I watched as his pulse throbbed in the hollow of his throat and I waited for his next exhalation. I lifted my hand toward this place of vulnerability, wanting to lay my fingers on it, to feel his heartbeat echo with mine, but I resisted the temptation to do so. Instead, I left my fingertips suspended above his steady pulse, hoping to calm my own thundering heartbeat.

I looked forward to sharing my life with this man. I raised my face a few inches from his, breathing in his breath, trying to convince myself that he was real . . . and mine, now and forever. All those years of searching could finally remain behind me. *What unforeseen series of events kept us from finding each other before now? What happenstance careened into motion of this cosmic universe that pulled us together at this time as if we were magnets slamming into each other's lives like a train wreck?* I mused to myself as I moved quietly to the edge of the bed. I sat still so as not to wake him, trying to remember what triggered the nightmare that I thought to be long gone.

Now, as my eyes looked around the dimly lit bedroom, I remembered. I walked to the wide, wooden slats of the shutters on the window and parted them just enough to let in a small slit of morning light. The painting hung on the wall opposite the bed so it was the last thing I looked at before I went to sleep, and the first thing I saw when I woke up. I moved to stand in front of the painting, still trying to focus my eyes to the adjusting light as it landed with white streaks across the canvas. Even now, as I stood in front of this beautiful scene of Arizona, with its craggy mountain face, desert trees, and serene-looking water, it drew me back to my childhood. *How did he manage to paint it looking so serene, when he knew what happened there years ago?* I wondered as an icy shudder quickly spread up the back of my neck, causing gooseflesh to appear on my skin.

Yes, that must be it. The painting brought back all those tragic memories of years ago. Maybe now . . . for the last time.

The drowning nightmare revisited me as a result of seeing Canyon Lake again in this beautiful painting. It's always the same. I am floating down in clear, blue water. It doesn't become a nightmare until I realize that I can't reach the surface; some force is holding me down. I keep struggling to ascend because I'm looking at the underside of a boat bobbing on the surface. I keep fighting to free myself and, just as I get close enough, a hand reaches down into the water, ready to pull me out. Our fingertips barely touch and I am shaken out of the dream, still gasping for breath as I wake in a panic.

"Rae, what's wrong? Come back to bed. I'm not ready to get up yet," his still sleepy voice said to me.

I gave a startled jump and tore my eyes away from the canvas. I turned to look into the steel-blue eyes and raven-black hair with threads of gray running through it, into the face of the man who saved me more than once from my terrors.

"Oh, yes you are," I said, looking at the tent-like shape rising under the crumpled sheets as I crawled back to him from the foot of the bed. I knew that we both found the happiness and peace of mind eluding us all these years.

After making love, my bed partner drifted back to sleep and I retreated to the back patio with a cup of hot green tea. I looked out over the morning desert. The aromas of creosote and dust took me back to that night in Scottsdale, where my life took an unexpected turn.

2

~ *Rae* ~

The Painting

I T'S JULY IN ARIZONA, not the best time for walking around and enjoying the sights. The air during the day is heavy with heat and little, if any, moisture. But for us desert-dwellers, you get used to it or you become a recluse and don't go out at all during the daylight hours. I always carry a bottle of water and wear a hat and, of course, the ever-present sunscreen. In the evening, however, the air carries the fragrant aroma of the desert. Even from town, if you close your eyes and lift your face upward, you can find a slight trail of scent filled with the pungent traces of creosote bushes and cactus blossoms. It is almost as if you are standing in a desert oasis instead of a street filled with the noises of traffic and people. On this particular evening, a friend and I decided to visit Scottsdale's ArtWalk in Old Town Scottsdale. This traditional event, every Thursday evening, showcases all the beautiful and unique artwork on display in the various galleries. I've made my home in the valley for over thirty years and have never made the time to go . . . now I went.

The Scottsdale Gallery Association hosts three special event art walks in addition to the weekly events. July is the Summer Spectacular, which hopes to encourage visitors to venture out into the desert night and escape the heat of the day.

In any case, my friend and I chose the July event to meander through the shops and galleries of downtown Scottsdale. We made our way in and out of several of the galleries, looking at all the current art trends and enjoying the occasional cheese tray and wine sample. My friend noticed one painting in particular near the door of a crowded, southwestern gallery. I already walked out the door and stood on the crowded sidewalk, waiting for him to join me. I was trying to find a safe place to stand, as people strolled by, not watching where they were going, but looking in the storefront windows of the galleries they passed. Once I found a place out of the way, I turned around to see what was keeping my friend and noticed him standing squarely in front of a painting in the gallery I had just left. My curiosity drew me back in to find out what captured his attention so suddenly. As I reentered the gallery and joined him in front of the painting, he asked, "Isn't this Canyon Lake?"

I looked more carefully and agreed that it did, in fact, appear to resemble a scene from Canyon Lake, a local recreational area. Even though many years had passed since being there, somewhere back in my memory the scene still existed. The artist nameplate with title confirmed it. I looked at it, stymied. My curiosity was piqued. *Who was this artist, and why did he choose Canyon Lake and this particular spot? Yes, the mountains remain beautiful even today, but the surrounding recreational area lingers with minimal amenities.* Now I knew . . . I needed this painting, and I had to find out the reason for its creation.

I asked my friend to wait while I went to find the gallery owner. Without realizing it, because of my absorption in the painting, the gallery teemed with people standing and looking at paintings and other artifacts. I saw two men, both engaged in separate conversations. One was medium height and dark haired with a few streaks of gray running though it. He stood listening, one arm folded across his chest supporting the other, to an animated young man talking and gesturing with his hands, trying to draw the man into conversation. He happened to look in my direction with deep, steel-blue eyes that I could not help but notice even from across the room. His glance went past me to the other man on the opposite side of the room. I followed the direction of his eyes and noticed a much taller and muscular man stepping away from a patron. His casual dress consisted of modern western wear that included polished western boots made of some exotic leather that I did not recognize and what I assumed to be, because of the size and amount of sterling silver used in its creation, a very expensive Native American bolo tie. He noticed my movement toward him at the same time as his friend made eye contact. I now came face-to-face with this imposing figure, as he stretched out his hand in greeting.

"Hello, I'm Lee Beck. Welcome to my gallery. Can I help you with anything?" A slow smile spread across his thoroughly masculine face and chiseled chin, revealing deep laugh lines beneath a day-old beard. It took me a moment to remember what I wanted to ask.

"Hi, I'm Rae Warner. I'm interested in this painting, *Canyon Lake*. What can you tell me about it and the artist? Do you know if he's local?" I took a few steps back as Mr. Beck approached me to stand in front of the painting.

"Yes, the artist resides here in the area. Would you like to see the other pieces of his work in the gallery?" He started to move away and direct me to another desert scene with similar lighting.

"No, Mr. Beck," I said, still standing in front of the painting. "I'm only interested in this one." I reached inside my shoulder bag for my pen and tore a piece of paper from the ArtWalk program. I wrote my name and address on it. "Would you mind giving this note to . . . ?" I looked closer at the name plate, "Mr. Sullivan when you see him again? I would like to talk with him. I'm sorry I can't stay longer, but I have a friend waiting for me. I'd like to come back next week and buy this painting if it's still available." I handed Lee Beck my scribbled note. "Thank you for your time, Mr. Beck." I started toward the door. For some reason I felt an urgency to leave, as if his hand might come to rest on my shoulder and prevent me from leaving.

"Ms. Warner, please call me Lee. I'll be sure Mr. Sullivan gets this." He held up my note as a wave goodbye. I went quickly out the door and found my companion patiently waiting for me at the curb next to his car.

"What's wrong?" he asked, as I hurriedly got in the car.

"Oh, it's nothing. I just had a strange feeling." I felt as if Mr. Beck's eyes saw more than my face. He seemed to give off this nefarious aura. I had this feeling once before, when I met the father of one of my students during parent conferences at school. I was to find out, years later, that the man had molested a friend of my student. I settled back and fastened my seat belt. I looked back at the gallery window and saw Lee Beck smiling at me, my note still in his hand. I hoped I hadn't made a mistake.

"The painting is beautiful. I told the gallery owner that I would be back next week to buy it. Let's go. I need something to drink." For some reason, the experience at the gallery left me shaken. *I shouldn't have given him my phone number; I should have made another visit in person.*

After my friend and I left the downtown area of Scottsdale, we headed toward home and made a short stop for one beer at our favorite place to go after work to unwind. I was hoping the beer would help me relax and forget, for the time being, about my earlier encounter with Mr. Beck.

Now, at home and settled into the safety of my own place, I began to think again about all those years ago at the lake. The brief encounter with this painting made me go back to that horrific day, only this time I was thinking about the man who pulled my parents out of the water and saved them from drowning.

We never knew his name or how he happened to find himself at this particular place in time. I had to find out more about this artist and why he chose to paint this precise scene. Surely, there could not be any connection . . .

3

~ *Joe* ~

The Opening

MY DAY STARTED EARLIER than usual because I volunteered to help Lee prepare the gallery for the opening. I felt especially hopeful about this as I drove into town from my combination home and studio in the foothills of the Superstition Mountains. This was to be my first professional showing and most of the work that was on exhibition, along with the music, was mine.

When I pulled up to the gallery and parked in front of the large picture window that displayed one of my earlier landscapes, Lee was sweeping the front entrance and looked up as I locked my Jeep and met him on the sidewalk.

"Good morning, Joe. How was your trip into town?"

"Morning, Lee. Oh, the ride in was great. The mornings are cool, with a lot less traffic."

"Well, come on in. I've got the coffee started. We can discuss our strategy while we are having our first cup." Lee held the door open for me as I walked through the cool gallery air. I still wasn't used to the cooler temperature that he kept in the gallery because of the artwork. The hot coffee would hit the spot until I got warmed up from all the exertion of the work ahead of me.

As the day progressed and we worked on hanging and re-hanging the paintings to show off their best light, it became apparent that I looked forward to the premier of my exhibit during this year's Scottsdale ArtWalk July Summer Spectacular. I became more nervous than I expected about exposing my art and music all at once. For Lee's sake and expense, I hoped for a good turnout.

The early summer night turned out to be a warm evening scented with subtle aromas of citrus and jasmine. These evening scents mixed with ones that flowed from flavored tea stands set up along the street for prospective patrons wandering in and out of galleries. Steel drums played outside where Marshall Way and Main Street met. Lee used one of my music CD's as background music in his gallery. The overall effect was quite relaxing, like visiting with old friends for a quiet evening.

Little did I know that this perfect mixture of sights, sounds, and aromas would produce a chance meeting, turning my world upside down.

Lee's gallery is usually open seven days a week during the winter months because of all the winter visitors that flock to the valley. However, during the summer months, he closes on Sunday. For the ArtWalk evenings, he stays open late or at least until all the prospective buyers receive the answers to their questions and any last possible sales are made.

Since this particular evening featured most of my work, I made it a point to support Lee and answer any inquiries that might come up. The gallery soon filled with many different types of people; from locals who never miss the event, to those from out of town who wanted something to do on a Thursday evening.

Lee hired a catering service to make sure the cheese and fruit trays, punch bowls, and wine cups were kept filled. He hoped the people would stay in the gallery longer and take their time looking in order to make that big purchase.

Doubts flooded my mind as to whether all this time and effort would be worth it. As of now, Lee sold several of my pieces, and many people asked if I did any commission work. I collected their names and phone numbers so I could set up appointments in the hopes of finding if their interests would prove to be genuine, along with the possibility of future projects.

At one point during the evening, I noticed a man and a woman talking together quietly in front of my *Canyon Lake* landscape. From where I stood, they looked like a local couple, not in flashy, trendy clothes, but dressed comfortably. She wore jeans that showed off her petite form, and her blonde, sun-kissed hair was in a coiled wrap, secured with a wooden pick. The man, not much taller than her, wore his long, blonde hair tied back under a baseball cap.

I saw the woman look around several times, as if to seek out someone who might answer a question. I spotted Lee turning in my direction just as he finished his conversation with a patron. He saw me look at the woman standing in front of my *Canyon Lake* painting and gave me a nod, then headed in her direction. I stood with arms across my chest, being deluged with questions from a first-year college art student wanting me to describe my techniques and style. By the time I could break free and start to make my way across the room, the man and woman had left the gallery. I started out the door in the hopes of still being able to catch them. The sidewalk bustled with casual gallery-goers. The man and woman became lost in the crowd. I glanced in both directions, but realized it was fruitless and stepped back inside the gallery. As the surge of activity began to dwindle and closing time approached, Lee and I slumped in chairs and started to take note of the evening's success.

"Well Joe . . . I'd say we did well enough for you to take a vacation, and I can go skiing in Colorado this season," Lee said, as he put his size eleven boots on his desk. I sat exhausted in an over-sized leather chair worn with age and nodded my head in agreement.

"I guess all my doubts were a little premature." My mind went back to that earlier couple I missed. "Hey Lee, did you happen to see that couple looking at *Canyon Lake*?"

Lee stretched and yawned while he said no.

"Now wait a minute." He reached in his pocket and took out a piece of paper. "A woman gave me this and said she would like to meet the artist who painted it. She also said she would be back in a couple of days to buy it if the painting's still available. She told me her name. Now, what was it?" Lee rubbed his hand over his face a few times. "Oh yeah, her name was Rae Warner. Do you know her?"

As he handed me the torn piece of paper from the

ArtWalk program, I asked, "Was she the small blonde with her hair tied in a knot?"

"Yeah, she was a real beauty. I love blue eyes and blonde hair," Lee replied as he stood, stretching, and began walking toward the front door, making ready to close up the gallery.

"Okay, okay. Easy boy," I said to Lee, then looked down at the note and absently read the neatly written words, "Are you the one who saved my parents?" I sat up in the chair and reread the words again. My hands began to shake and a terrifying scream echoed in my head. Lee came back into the room.

"Hey, buddy, you don't look so good. You must be more tired than I thought. You'd better go home and get some rest."

I stood, unsure if I could get my legs to work, and took a step toward the front door, crushing the note in my hand as I went. I said my goodbyes to Lee and thanked him for all his work. When I reached the Jeep, my mind reeled. *Could this woman have some connection to that long ago nightmarish event? Could she somehow be linked to that near drowning couple? Or, God forbid, does she know something about what happened to my stepfather? No . . . she can't know. She didn't look old enough to have been there. I blocked out all these memories years ago, I thought, leaving the horror of it behind me. I've finally put my life back together. I can't go through this again.*

4

~ *Joe* ~

The Meeting

THE DAYS FOLLOWING MY show were filled with many up and down emotions. Lee called and said the evening event was deemed a success by his standards. Enough of my paintings and CDs sold to ensure my future success as a local artist and helped to establish a solid foothold for future showings. Lee excitedly announced that several local business owners wanted to talk to me about possible projects for murals. A school district administrator expressed an interest in starting an artist in residence program working with elementary-aged students, and several reporters covering the event wanted interviews.

Fortunately for me, Lee is a good enough friend not to give out my phone number. He cheerfully told them he would forward their requests to me and that Mr. Sullivan's agent would contact them. What a surprise; I didn't know I had an agent. However, if business continued to escalate, I might need an agent after all.

A week after the opening, I resumed my routine of painting and composing the best I could, in light of the recent surge in activity. I became more curious about the note left by the blonde woman at the opening. It could only mean some sort of a coincidence. What else is there? The best outcome I could hope for would be for her to forget about the painting and not buy it. As much as I needed to sell my work, a feeling of apprehension came over me and suggested that I let this possibility go by the wayside. I could not afford to let any recurring nightmares interfere with my creative processes at this point in my career.

Early the next morning, I found myself working in my studio, doing a bit of cleaning up. An assortment of scattered brushes, paint rags, and framed canvases lay in disarray around the workroom. Cupboard doors, left open during a search for materials, exposed various art supplies and tools. While working on an art project or music, I tend to let the clean up go until I have finished with a particular project. Living alone, I can afford myself the luxury of not having to pick up after myself. I pushed myself to get ready to start a new series of landscape pieces from the sketches I made on a recent trip to Texas and New Mexico. When Lee phoned from the gallery early in the afternoon, I realized I was ready to take a break from my tumult of activity.

His voice sounded different from his usual friendly tone and I didn't recognize him at first. "Joe, this is Lee. Do you remember the woman who was interested in your *Canyon Lake* painting, Rae Warner?"

"Lee, what's wrong, where are you? You sound like you're in a cave."

"Oh, sorry Joe, I'm in the back room. I didn't want

her to hear me talking to you. Well, do you remember her or not?" Lee spoke in a clearer voice.

"Well, yeah. Does she want the painting?" I found myself holding my breath, while curiosity swirled in my head.

"Yes, she's already bought it. She asked me what I knew about the artist. She wanted to know if you live in the area and if you own your own studio. I told her, 'yes, he's local and he lives and works in his studio so it's not open to the public,'" Lee blurted out before taking a breath. "I told her I'd call you and she could talk to you herself."

"You told her that? Oh damn, Lee. I can't talk to her. I'm in the middle of a big project."

"Sorry if I screwed up, but I didn't think you would mind. She seems harmless, and she told me that Canyon Lake holds special memories for her because she almost lost her family there," Lee explained.

"Okay, if you already told her." I took several deep breaths and told myself to relax. *This can't be happening. She can't know anything about any of this.* In the background I heard the general stirrings of the gallery and then footsteps approaching the phone.

"Hello, Mr. Sullivan, this is Rae Warner. Thank you for taking the time to talk with me. I admire your work very much," said a pleasant, very definite female voice. There was a trace of hesitancy in her voice and I waited for her to finish.

"Well, thank you." I felt my heart skip a beat. "I'm glad you enjoy my work. I think I saw you and a companion looking at *Canyon Lake*. I apologize for not getting over to you before you left the gallery. You looked as if you had some questions," I said, realizing I was talking too fast.

"Yes. I came with a friend of mine. May I ask how you came to paint this particular scene? I've never seen a painting of Canyon Lake before. It doesn't seem like a typical Arizona place to paint a landscape," Ms. Warner said in a hesitant, slightly quivering voice.

"I really don't know why I painted it, it just came to me after I visited the area." I didn't really want to tell her why I painted it just yet.

"Oh . . . then, you're not the one." She said it so softly, I could barely hear her voice tinged with disappointment.

"Excuse me, Ms. Warner, but I was given a note from the ArtWalk night. Did you leave it with Mr. Beck? What does it mean? I'd like to know, if you can tell me." I realized she might hang up and then I would never know.

"Yes, I'm the one. You probably think I'm crazy, but can you tell me if you ever visited Canyon Lake about thirty years ago and helped a family in trouble?"

Rae's voice now became full of hope as she waited for my reply. *How did this happen? After all these years, how did this woman walk into Lee's gallery and buy my painting?* My mind swam as I realized I had been holding my breath and my hands began to sweat. I let it out in a blast of relief and said, "No, I'm sorry, Ms. Warner, I can't help you. I really must go now. I'm in the middle of several projects I must complete in order to meet my deadline. I'm sure Mr. Beck can help you if you need any more information. Can you please put Mr. Beck back on the phone? Thank you, Ms. Warner. It's been a pleasure talking with you."

"Yes, Mr. Sullivan. I'm sorry to have bothered you. I'll get Mr. Beck for you." There was a long pause on the other end. So long, in fact, I thought she'd hung up the phone by mistake.

She didn't say anything, but I could hear voices in the background and Lee's heavy-booted footsteps approaching the phone.

"Joe, what the hell did you say to her? She's white as a ghost and her hands were shaking so bad I had to sit her in a chair." Lee's voice clearly depicted concern.

"Lee, I can't explain it all right now, but please don't give her anymore information. Did she take the painting with her?"

"Well, no. She wants a nameplate made for it and mounting clips. I told her I'd have it ready for her to pick up tomorrow. She's coming back for it in the afternoon."

"Okay, thanks. I'll talk to you soon." After I hung up, I felt sick. *Why did I treat her that way? She's only trying to find answers to something that apparently means a lot to her. She couldn't possibly have anything to do with this nightmare. Her voice didn't sound old enough to be the woman I pulled out of the water. God forbid she was one of those screaming kids on the shore watching her parents drown.*

After hanging up the phone, I wandered into my living room and slumped into a chair. Staring through my large picture window, my thoughts brought me back thirty years ago to that hot summer day when I pulled a man, a woman, and a small boy out of the water.

5

~ *Joe* ~

The Man

I BEGAN HELPING MY BUDDIES unload the car of the usual provisions for a day at the lake—an ice chest filled with beer and a few store-bought sandwiches. I asked myself, *Why am I here? I've got a research paper due and midterms coming up. I have too much schoolwork to do. I can't afford to take a day off. Why did I let Eddie and Tom talk me into this? Yes, the cool lake water is refreshing and the warm Arizona sun worked its magic to clear the cobwebs from my cluttered mind, but this twinge of guilt is making me feel uneasy. Is it because I have too much to do or is it some other reason?*

We found a spot under a big mesquite tree to store our ice chest. It should keep our snacks and beer cold until we decide to come out of the cold lake water. We each grabbed our over-sized inner tubes and headed for the water. The water did not have a fast enough current to carry us far, so we hand-paddled out to the middle and floated until we were pushed by the waves of a passing boat.

"Hey, check it out!" I heard Eddie yell from behind

and turned in time to see a boat cruise by with three bi-kini-clad girls. Tom and Eddie had already begun hand paddling toward the boat. By this time, I had already floated beyond hearing, but I could see them waving for me to come back. The three girls had stopped their boat and Tom and Eddie were climbing on board.

I could have turned around and made my way back toward Eddie and Tom, but for some reason I didn't feel like spending time with a crowd. I lay back in my tube and sank deeper into the water. I could hear the boat motor surge and take off upstream. Soon, I heard nothing and began to mindlessly drift away from where I left Eddie and Tom tubing. Before I realized it, my floating tube of relaxation bobbed its way near a small cove. Because it was a weekday instead of the weekend, I was pleasantly surprised to find very few tubers in this area. It looked like mostly families with young kids and a few other smaller clusters of people enjoying a midweek break. It was hardly worth the effort to make a trip to the lake on weekends because it tended to be so crowded with picnickers and noisy with boat motors.

With the gentle tug of the current made by passing boats, I began to settle into an atmosphere of peace and quiet, with the sun just starting to bead up my skin with sweat. Through the din of other distant voices of pic-nickers and boaters, the sheer screams of children star-tled me out of my reverie. I sat up with a jerk, splashing cold water over my sunburnt torso, and craned my neck, trying to pinpoint the screams. At first I couldn't locate where the screams originated from because the sounds came at me from all directions, bouncing off the canyon walls. At last my attention focused on four small children huddled together, clutching one another, and facing the water's edge. While my mind registered alarm, my body became tense with adrenaline, and I half swam, half ran to the shore as my sandaled feet found their footing on the rocky bottom. *Oh, God*, I thought to myself and scrambled to the shore, *this can't be happening again.*

A distant memory flashed through my mind, which made the bile rise up in my throat, but I swallowed it back down. I kept my eyes on the screaming kids as I struggled against the water and made my way to shore.

The children stood huddled together downstream from where I came on shore. I regained my solid footing and raced toward them. As I got closer to them, my eyes followed the directions of their terrifying screams for help.

Not far from the water's edge, within reaching distance, a man struggled in the water. His struggle, I found out later, became compounded by the fact that not only was he in trouble, but he had clasped a woman by the arm and clutched a boy between his legs.

As I approached to help, the man's head broke the surface and I yelled, "Give me your hand." Somehow I managed to dig my feet into the rocky soil to steady myself and pull both him and the woman out of the water at the same time. To my shocked surprise, a small boy also emerged from between the man's legs as I dragged them ashore.

As all three escaped from the water, I saw them begin breathing on their own. Somehow I remained on my feet during the sudden exertion, but soon felt my knees turn to jelly. I needed to sit down. The small boy was picked up by another man, who I thought must be some member of his family. The man, who I had just pulled from the water, was breathing heavily and helping the woman sit upright. She was pale and trembling, but was able to clear the water out of her lungs with a few good coughs. By this time, I was able to stand and steady myself. I did not get a good look at them and could not tell their ages, but the four young children stopped their screaming when they saw the man and woman being pulled out of the water. I could only assume they were their parents because, as I turned away and headed down the shoreline, I looked over my shoulder to see them standing together in a circle of stunned relief.

Only the taller child, a girl, lifted her face to look in my direction as I continued to make my way back down the rocky shore. Her face expressed the paleness of shock, as if she herself had been pulled from the water. I thought I saw a slight lift of her hand in my direction as a show of thanks, but I knew that look. It was a look of desperation and panic that had been on my face when I was much younger and in a similar situation. Now I understood it as only an unconscious reaction. I was in shock myself and found my hands shaking. I needed to regain my breath and composure. I turned to head back the way I came, slowly trying to get my legs to walk without trembling. I began looking for Eddie and Tom. *How far had I drifted in that tube?*

After walking on not yet stable legs, I found them on shore about a mile from where we started tubing. They sat together enjoying a cold beer and a sandwich in the sun when I came up to them and said, "Hey, it's time to go." They both looked up at me in surprise and began gathering up all their gear. My face must have shown distress because neither one of them asked me why at that moment, for which I was thankful.

"Sure, Joe, whatever you say. Eddie and me were thinking the same thing." I saw a look pass between them, but it didn't surface into a spoken question. The three of us have known each other enough years to know when not to ask questions. At that moment, I probably could not have found the words to describe what just took place. I needed to sort it all out myself first. This episode became almost like deja vu all over again, only this time it had a happier ending.

I drove my car to the lake that day. I loved that car. I made a good deal on it before I started college; it was my prized possession. My dream car was a 1962 Chevy Nova, two-tone brown, bucket seats, and baby-moon hubcaps. Tom and Eddie considered it a real "girl-getter" and drove it as much as I did. They obviously experienced better results with it than me. They were known around campus for their party exploits. I remained more reclusive despite their insistence that I join them on their weekend parties.

On the way home, however, Tom drove and Eddie rode shotgun, while I collapsed in the backseat. I remember them talking in hushed tones, wondering what the hell happened back there, but I already began fading to black under the fog of exhaustion and bewilderment. As we got into town I began to wake up. My body felt like I finished swimming a marathon. When we pulled into the dorm parking lot at the campus of Arizona State University, Tom and Eddie stopped talking to each other and wanted to know what happened. Since we all lived in the same dorm, it would be difficult for me to avoid discussing the situation.

Fortunately for me, Tom and Eddie didn't need much of an explanation. They suggested we go to the Memorial Union (MU, as it is called) to play some pool. I said, "Let's go." The last thing I wanted to do right then was to dwell on the afternoon's events.

"Tell me about the girls on the boat. Did you get their numbers?" I tried to ease into the conversation.

"Forget about the girls, we want to know what shook you up. And, yeah, we got their numbers. We may even share them with you, if you let us in on your afternoon adventure," Tom said with a slight smirk on his face. The smirk soon disappeared from both their faces when I related my harrowing experience.

I told them briefly that some people got into trouble near the shore and I helped them get out.

"Hey, man, you're a hero!" Eddie said, followed by Tom's familiar slap on the back.

That brief explanation seemed to satisfy them and they didn't question me further. I was thankful because I needed some time to come to terms with the closeness of the experience, as well as with the one I lived through many years ago.

6

~ *Joe* ~

The Journey

MY COLLEGE YEARS CAME and went, basically un-eventful. Not being a jock, my remaining options became partying, academics, and girls. I did very little social partying and had few dates; that left only academics. In between studying and preparing to finish my teaching degree, I still made time for my art and music.

I remember, growing up as a kid, wanting to be a policeman. My dad was a cop, but was killed while on duty when I was ten. My mother had to go to work to support me and my younger sister, Lou. She never encouraged me to follow my dad in police work, but instead put a paintbrush in my hand. In my early teen years I discovered the guitar and found that I was good at both painting and music.

During my time in college, I completed several Southwest landscapes which helped finance my tuition. I found, over the years, that the Southwest provided a variety of artistic venues. Being a transplant from the Northwest, I came to love the desert. I never grew tired of the heat and the endless sunsets that most artists can never truly recreate, no matter how hard they try.

My music continued to progress and became an important part of my life. As an artist, I am always surprised to find new inspiration for my music and art. I meet occasionally with several music friends and we try out our latest licks. I knew I probably would never become a professional musician, but I enjoyed it and used it as an emotional and spiritual release to accompany my artwork.

After graduating from ASU, I landed a job teaching high school English and art in a local school district. My daily challenge became finding new ways to motivate high school kids to express themselves in writing and art. My students always exhibited an abundance of emotional energy to draw from, but helping them find a positive way to deal with it became the tough part.

Through my teaching years, I continued with my own desire to paint and began to sell a few pieces at local art shows. Several of my friends and buyers began to encourage me to open a studio of my own and devote full time to painting and songwriting. After ten years of teaching, I started to think more seriously about making the change from teacher to full-time artist and musician. Through some good advice and sound investments over the years, I saved some money and decided now would be a good time to give it a try. Given the fact that I was not married and had no children to support, I was free to make the decision to open my own studio. I looked forward to having a wife some day and possibly children, but for now it looked like it would not be happening anytime soon. Within a few weeks, I was in the hunt for a combination studio and house.

7

~ *Joe* ~

The Gallery

I DECIDED TO START LOOKING for a bigger house, one with a large enough space that could be used as a studio or, with a little remodeling, could have one built on.

My sister, Lou, said she knew of a house that might be available. A friend of hers from college planned on moving back east and needed to sell her house and half acre lot. She made arrangements for us to meet her friend, Sue, at the house the next Saturday.

The house itself was situated on the outskirts of town, faced east, and had a glorious view of the Superstition Mountains. I thought this opportunity might be too good to be true. Why would anyone want to leave a place like that? It sounded perfect for me. Sue, however, didn't share my feelings. She inherited it from her aunt who recently passed away. She was tired of the desert heat and became homesick for the east.

As we pulled up into the circular, gravel driveway, I sat back to take in the quiet, old house surrounded by the grandeur of the mountains. Like an artist's canvas, these mountains became the backdrop in a completed landscape.

"Hi Sue. Thanks for meeting us here. I'd like you to meet my brother, Joe. He's the one I told you about. He's looking for a place to use as his live-in studio."

"Hi, it's nice to meet you. Come on in. Sorry, but it's going to be hot in here. I had the electricity and water turned off after I put it up for sale." Sue met us as we got out of the car and we followed her up the gravel driveway through the natural desert landscape into the house.

After Sue had shown us through the house, Lou and her friend reminisced outside on the patio; I wandered back through the house. Even though it was weathered with age, it appeared to be in generally good shape. It would need a couple of coats of paint and a good cleaning, understandably so since no one had lived there for years.

A huge picture window looked out at the mountains and desert. Two smaller rooms toward the back of the house would make a great studio after removing a wall. Plenty of morning light for painting would be available through oversized windows. Acoustically it would be perfect for my music.

Before we left, I assured Sue that I wanted the house. I made arrangements to meet her at the realtor's office to sign papers as soon as they were available.

And so it began. I settled quickly into the quiet peace of finding one's own space. I worked on the house, doing minor repairs and painting, in between writing music and working on sketches. The house took on an airy, open atmosphere, which inspired my creative flow.

Before I knew it, I had completed three canvases, and wrote the lyrics and composed music for two songs.

As I began to become part of my surroundings, I ventured out and wanted to explore more of this beautiful desert. One of my favorite trips became hiking the Peralta Trail up in the Superstition Mountains. Being a novice hiker, it was one of the easier and well-used trails in these formidable mountains. Over the years, the Superstition Mountains became one of my many inspirations and favorite respites.

Several of my friends asked if I'd been to Tortilla Flats since I showed a keen interest in mountains and deserts. When I said no, a look of surprise crept over their faces. Needless to say, my curiosity was piqued and away I went. I got my well-used maps and discovered it would be a pleasant car trip through the mountains on Route 88, heading northeast. My faithful Nova, from my college years, had seen better days. Because of my forays into wilderness areas, I needed a more suitable mode of transportation, so I bought a Jeep a few years earlier. It went where I needed to go on my treks. The Jeep proved to be just what I needed to haul my equipment and materials for painting and my instruments for writing music.

I awoke early one Saturday morning and began gathering the few things I wanted to take on my day trip. A few water bottles, a couple of apples from my kitchen, and a granola bar would make a sufficient snack for later. I needed a fresh sketchbook and walked into the studio to retrieve one and a few drawing pencils. As a photographer carries his camera, I carry my sketchbook everywhere. The other day, I made sure the Jeep had a full tank of gas, so I headed for the door and set out on a journey that would unknowingly change my life.

The sun was just coming up and I caught glimpses of it as I drove up and around the hills. It soon became apparent, as I left the desert floor and climbed in elevation; I was less aware of the scenery and become more focused on the road. If you've ever experienced driving in the mountains, it is one you will not soon forget. This little road trip became quite different from all other mountain roads I have experienced. Route 88 is approximately twelve miles of hairpin, serpentine turns that motorcycle enthusiasts travel on the weekends just for thrills. I am sure the scenery was breathtaking, but I saw very little of it. My eyes were glued to the small patch of road in front of me, trying to see around the next curve.

I am sure one day I will make the complete trip to Tortilla Flats, but on this day, I slowed to a stop by the sudden appearance of a sign post that read, "Canyon Lake." As I approached this recreational area, my eyes no longer looked at the road, but wandered up to the immense canyon walls coming into view. I made a hasty turn into the parking area and found a spot, even though it was a busy Saturday morning.

I suddenly forgot about my original destination and was totally awestruck by what loomed in front of me. The canyon walls before me dazzled with the most amazing formations and color spectrums. I got out of the Jeep and walked along the shore. Such as it was, some distant familiarity suddenly struck my consciousness that I thought I had forgotten. All those past years came streaming back and floated to the surface of my mind like a recurring dream. I shook my head and closed my eyes, pushing back the memories. I was not yet willing to face them again. Throughout my growth as an artist, painting and music became a positive outlet for me when past, unpleasant events seemed to creep back into the edges of my mind.

I found a shady spot free from debris in which to sit and started making some sketches. I sat there, letting my hand wander over the paper; I hoped that by painting this area I would find the release I needed.

I had become lost in my work for the next several hours, when the piercing screams of children broke through, shattering my peace. My eyes focused on children playing and splashing in the water, but those screams of excitement chilled my heart. I was temporarily sent back in time . . . back to that life-saving day many years ago. Rarely during the day am I troubled by the image of two near-drowned adults huddled among four children. It is during my sleep that I feel like I'm drowning and wake up struggling for breath.

My hands began to tremble and I could not hold my pencil. I shook off the slight tremor and, with determined concentration, began drawing the canyon wall in more detail. It seemed to help push away the terrified screams for help of those four young children, as well as my own personal nightmare.

8

~ *Joe* ~

The Image

LATER THAT DAY, BACK at home in the cool comfort of my studio, I looked at the sketches I made earlier at the lake. I surprised myself to find a different intensity and detail in those drawings.

I left my sketchbook on the table in the studio and headed for the patio, grabbing my guitar as I went. Music had always been my solace when I was troubled about something. And I was troubled about my recent experience at the lake. *Why had I not connected this place to what had happened years ago? It's hard to believe I could completely forget about that traumatic day.* This recent road trip triggered a flood of memories and I needed to step away from it and clear my mind. My music would help me.

After several days I went back to my sketches, scattered on my worktable where I had left them, and tried to make some sense out of the drawings I made of Canyon Lake. I carried them to the large picture window in my studio and stared down at them as if I had never seen them before. During that Saturday afternoon,

I filled many pages with renderings I don't remember doing. I turned back to the center of the studio and tossed them on the worktable, wondering what I was going to do with them. I began to see the lake in my mind's eye more clearly now and my plan to paint a scene finally came together after many weeks of restless wanderings and fitful nights. The images of four young children screaming for someone to help their drowning parents kept replaying in my mind until I thought I would go insane. Concentrating on turning my sketches into paintings seemed to help. The more I painted, the more settled I became. Eventually, I finished the three pieces and my sense of well-being returned, as well as sleeping through the night.

It struck me as odd that I never really thought much about this event after it happened. Years later, I often wondered about what happened to that family and young boy. I hoped they were able to put that near-tragic day behind them. My friends, Eddie and Tom, asked me about it again a few months later, but I couldn't recall much of what took place. The whole thing seemed like a dream. Maybe it wasn't me, but someone else who managed to save three people from drowning. I still, to this day, can't imagine how I did it. I am not an exceptionally strong man. I do, however, try to keep in shape and eat right, but I would never have believed I could have done what I did if it had not been for the unusual circumstances. Now, as I think back, I wonder how I ever managed to pull two adults and one young boy out of the water at the same time. I can only imagine it was one of those rare instances when fear and adrenalin take over and a person is able to do extraordinary things. Maybe I was given an opportunity to make up for what I couldn't do for my own family.

After I completed the landscapes, my gallery-owner friend, Lee Beck, approached me and suggested that I hang my work in his gallery. I could not be sure if any of them would sell, but they probably had a better chance in his place than my out-of-the-way studio.

Over the years, Lee's friendship became a great source of encouragement for me. We met shortly after I moved into my studio. I happened to be in Scottsdale, going through the galleries, trying to get ideas for my studio, when I met Lee. I wandered into his gallery and was immediately struck by the local flair and desert landscapes. We spent several hours talking shop. He said he started his new gallery deliberately featuring new local artists and wanted to know if I was interested in hanging a few of my paintings in his gallery.

"Good afternoon, welcome to my gallery. It looks like we're going to have another hot one," Lee's voice said from behind me. My attention was diverted by a deep-throated, gruff voice coming from somewhere to my left.

"Yes, thank God you have air conditioning. Do you have much trouble keeping the temperature and humidity regulated in your gallery?" I asked.

"No, it hasn't been much of a problem yet. When I first opened, I had a few problems, but now that the techs finally got the bugs worked out with the controls, everything works great. What kind of medium do you use?" He fired the question at me.

"Medium? How did you know I paint?" I asked, with a suspicious tone in my voice.

"Oh, I know the look, having been there myself. I used charcoal before I gave up and moved here to open the gallery. Now, I do what I can to promote new local artists."

"Yes, I see what you mean." While walking around the gallery, I did not recognize any names on the nameplates. "I use acrylic and oils. Mostly landscapes, a few stills. I just moved into a new place that I work out of," I replied.

"I'd be interested in seeing what you've got. Why don't you bring in a few pieces to hang here? See what happens," Lee suggested.

"You sure you wouldn't mind?"

"Sure, why not? Our next ArtWalk around here is coming up at the end of the month. It would be a good time to see if your work would generate some interest and any new patrons."

"Okay. I'll bring in a few pieces for you to look at. Give you a feel for the kind of work I do," I said.

Through my business dealings with Lee, I came to find out he was not your stereotypical Southwest gallery owner. He's originally from Colorado and moved to Scottsdale after his own lackluster art career was put on hold. I've never heard him say why he left Colorado and it hasn't come up in our conversations again, so I never thought to ask. After his first awestruck visit to the Southwest, he became hooked like me and stayed to open his own gallery. He has never talked about his family and I never asked. We haven't shared any of the personal aspects of our lives and spend most of our conversations talking about art and music. He keeps to himself and we work well together. Lee possesses self-assurance and confidence that immediately puts you at ease. I am sure women are highly attracted to him, not only for his rugged exterior, but because he looks like he just stepped out of an Eddie Bauer catalog with a southwest touch. Each time I see him he's wearing tastefully expensive western boots and a handcrafted Native American bolo tie that is always loosely strung around his neck.

Lee's busy gallery has been successful for me over the years. To my surprise, several of my paintings sold within the first six months. Two of my Canyon Lake scenes, depicting different canyons and water lines, sold shortly afterwards. The third Canyon Lake painting, showing a larger canyon face and lagoon area, remained in the Scottsdale gallery for a year-and-a-half before I took it back to my studio. I included it in my last showing, which happened to be the one Rae Warner purchased. *God, why did she have to buy that one?*

I continue to paint and extend my circle of traveling to other southwest states. New Mexico and Texas also offered me many new scenic sights and inspirations for my painting, as well as my music. The Southwest deserts seemed to provide the creative muse that I need.

Over the years my two crafts coexisted and became similar in mood, theme, and vision. Lee suggested we promote my CDs and sell them along with the paintings. It became a profitable venture and it enabled me to enjoy my newfound lifestyle.

I've done more traveling around the U.S. and even made a trip to Mexico. Each trip became a beneficial experience for me because it helped to enrich my painting and music. I began picking up more and more of the southwest style, and its subtle nuances came out in my paintings and music.

Fortunately, I never needed to worry about leaving my studio unattended. My sister, Lou, and her kids, Mallory, a very grown-up twelve-year-old who has developed an interest in drawing, much to the liking of her uncle, and Sage, a rambunctious ten-year-old who wants to learn to play the guitar. Lou told me that she would use her quiet time to catch up on her reading. The three of them came anytime I needed them, making it their home away from home. They all knew, of course, after a brief orientation, that the studio was off limits because many of my pieces are works in progress. I never stayed away too long because the Arizona desert and my studio always drew me back.

"Joe, remember you promised the kids to start them on their lessons. Sage is ready to start guitar lessons with you. Ever since you bought him the guitar for Christmas, he has picked away at it everyday. He's already been through the lesson books you gave him, twice. He's asked me about taking lessons at school," Lou reminded me.

"I know Lou. I'm sorry. I've just been preoccupied with getting my studio set up and getting pieces to Lee's gallery. As soon as I get back from my trip, I'll set up a schedule to work with Sage after school," I said.

"Don't forget about Mallory. She's taking art this semester as an elective. Her teachers say that she's doing very well. She has a creative mind and a keen eye for detail in her drawings. Joe, she's so excited about talking to you," Lou added.

"I've noticed that, too, Lou. She has shown me a few

sketches and they show a nice flair. I think, with the right training, she can develop the potential to create some interesting work," I said.

I only planned to be gone a few weeks. Just a short break from the hectic schedule I felt myself under since committing to hanging my work in Lee's gallery.

I've always been close to Lou, especially since the loss of her father—my stepfather. Over the years, we became even closer after her divorce, and I was there to help, when I could, with the kids. As I remained un-married, she willingly let me step in as a surrogate fa-ther. At this point in her children's lives, it became more important than ever to remain close to them, especially since they were just now developing their own sense of creativity and personal expression. I always want to remain connected to them and be a part of their lives.

Up until this time, I devoted twenty years plus to my painting, music, and traveling. It was not a conscious choice, just something that happened. I dated occa-sionally and met new people by way of publishing my music, showing my art, and traveling. I was happy and somewhat content, but a nagging feeling that I needed more in my life seemed to hang over me at times. In the back of my mind I always thought I would get married and have children, but it was not an all-driving force. I enjoyed being around Lou and her kids. They were great kids and were always ready for an adventure.But I admit, the older I became, the more the thought of marriage crossed my mind.

This was the first time in my life where I felt ready to think about getting married. Lou adjusted well after her divorce and the kids were doing fine in school. She was too young to remember losing her father that day at the lake. I was barely old enough to swim myself. When I think back about it now, I was only twelve. What could I have done differently? That nagging thought still comes to me, even now. *If only I could have saved him.*

9

~ Rae ~

The Hunt

DURING MY LAST VISIT to the gallery, I made arrangements with Mr. Beck to return the next day to pick up the painting. He assured me that the nameplate would be ready, and to come in any time after two o'clock. I sat in my car, parked in front of the entrance to the gallery, and read a sign that said "Closed". *Great,* I thought, looking down at my watch. *It's already two-fifteen and I have to be across town by three. What do I do now? He didn't give me his card, so I can't leave a message on his machine. I'll wait a few more minutes and then leave a note on the door.*

I sat with my windows open, watching the afternoon shoppers. The morning coolness was quickly turning into afternoon heat. The sidewalks were crowded with people meandering in and out of shops, but it was not as busy as the night of the ArtWalk. I couldn't help thinking about how strange this all was, that I came to be at this gallery, waiting to pick up my first piece of expensive art. First, I happened across this painting and then, when I find the artist, he doesn't seem to want to talk to me. The gallery owner, Lee Beck, is undoubtedly handsome with a mesmerizing glint in his eyes, but he left me in a quandary. There was something about him, though, I couldn't quite put my finger on it. It's as if he knew my vulnerable spot and was waiting for it to be exposed.

I continued to wait, unconsciously rubbing my wrists and staring off into nothingness.

A sudden change in light across the windshield of my car shifted my attention back to the store window. I could see movement toward the back of the gallery and a small light come on. It must be a desk lamp. I leaned forward, shading my eyes with my hand to try to get a better look at what was going on in the gallery. Sitting back, I let out the breath I was holding and remained in my car, waiting for whoever it was to come to the front and unlock the door. It must be Mr. Beck because I can now see a large man picking up the phone and beginning a conversation. Oh, great! There goes another ten minutes. Soon, though, he finished and came to the front of the gallery. He saw me sitting in my car and motioned me in. I got out of my car, paused to stretch my legs, and then locked the door. He walked out of the gallery, stepped to the curb, and helped me into the chilly, air-conditioned gallery. The place smelled of fresh paint, turpentine, and a slight scent of something else I couldn't quite place.

"Oh, Ms. Warner, I'm so sorry to keep you waiting. Something unexpected came up. Please forgive me. Can I get you some water?" he said, taking my arm and leading me to a plush leather chair by his desk, similar to the one I sat in after my distressing conversation with Mr. Sullivan a few days earlier.

"No thank you, Mr. Beck. I just came by to pick up *Canyon Lake*. I hope it's ready. I can't stay long, I have another appointment."

"Please, call me Lee. May I call you Rae? I hope we can be friends now that you are a patron of the arts. I am so pleased that this painting found a home, and especially by you. Joe completed it several years ago and gave up thinking it would ever sell. I knew it would all along. It was only a matter of time, and finding the right buyer. You seemed very taken with it, Rae," Lee said, as I watched his eyes travel from my head to my feet, leaving me with a very uneasy feeling.

"Yes Lee, I am very taken with it. I knew the minute I saw it that I needed to have it. This is my first big art purchase and I'm very excited to be able to buy it. I only wish that I hadn't offended Mr. Sullivan. I would really like to talk to him. Tell me, Lee, what do you know about him? Is there any background on the painting that you know of?" As I spoke to him, Lee rose from his chair behind the desk and moved around the room, as if he needed more time to think before he answered. He came back to sit at his desk again and looked intently into my face.

"Well Rae, I don't know too much. I met Joe when I opened my gallery a few years ago. We helped each other get settled into this art world business. He keeps pretty much to himself, same as me. Would you mind me asking you something?"

His sudden question startled me. When I didn't respond right away, he proceeded to ask, "What does

Canyon Lake mean to you? I mean, it seems important to you in some way."

"I'm sorry, Mr. Beck," I said looking, down at my watch. "I really must be going. I have to be across town soon." I stood and started to make my way to the door.

"No, Rae, I'm the one who should apologize. It's none of my business. You can buy any painting you want, it doesn't matter why. Please forgive me. I seem to be starting out on the wrong foot with you." His expression and demeanor were quite woeful, like that of a child caught in the act of telling a lie.

"That's all right. Don't worry about it. Thank you for wrapping up my new piece of art. I can't wait to take it home." I stood, waiting at the unopened door, as I didn't want to face the heat outside until the last possible moment.

"Rae, I know this may sound brash, but would you be interested in having dinner with me sometime? I would like to make up for all my faux pas." He now placed his hand over mine as it held the cold, metal door handle.

I looked up into his face and saw a sweet smile and twinkling eyes. How could I resist? A sudden chill ran up the back of my neck. I ignored it and stammered on.

"Oh yes, that would be fine. You have my number, call any time. Oh, by the way, would you give this letter to Mr. Sullivan the next time you see him? Thanks." I moved my hand from the handle and Lee opened the door.

I stepped out into the hot Arizona afternoon and the heat blasted my face. I sat in my car, which had become quite hot as the early afternoon sun streamed in the windows, and yet a chill crept over me and made me shiver. I shook it off and started to drive away. Looking back in my rearview mirror, I saw Lee standing at the window of the door, waving at me with my letter to Mr. Sullivan in his hand. It was the same grin I saw on his face the night of the ArtWalk.

Back in the cool, dimness of the gallery, Lee returned to his desk. He sat, looking at the envelope in his hand with the neat-scripted name of Joe Sullivan written on the front. The smile on his face this time was not one of sweetness, but of maliciousness.

He said aloud to no one, "Yeah, I'll give it to him as soon as I read it. What am I, his messenger? He made it clear that he didn't want anything to do with you, bitch." He tossed the envelope with a flick of his hand, landing it on top of a pile of paperwork stacked haphazardly on his desk. He left it there while he walked back to the rear of the gallery and into the workroom. He found one remaining beer left in the small refrigerator and stood staring at the black, enamel-painted door. He swung opened the heavy metal door of the vault and made his way down the stairs into the cool, semi-darkness of the lower level under the gallery. "I think I'll close up shop early today. I've got some unfinished business to take care of," he said to himself.

10

~ *Rae* ~

The Lake

Accelerating away from Main Street and the gallery, with my treasure safely wrapped, I headed east toward home. The other errands I had planned for the day could wait. My visit with Lee Beck left me unsettled and I wanted to get my painting home in a safe place. For some unexplained reason, I thought it might vanish before me like a dream. Without realizing it, I found myself parked on the gravel driveway, looking at the front terrace of my house. I sat for a moment, enjoying the relief of being home. I loved this house, it was all mine. It was the one and only thing I wanted from my divorce. Robert couldn't understand why I wanted to live way out here by myself. He suggested that we sell the house and the acre plot and split the money. I stood my ground for once and said I wanted it. He was surprised by my determination and acquiesced, signing over the deed. We owned the land and house free and clear, so I was relieved not to have a house payment to worry about. It was going to be some time before I would get my finances in shape once the divorce was final, but, again, I was determined to do this on my own.

I managed to slide the wooden, two-by-two-foot frame carefully from my backseat, making my way to the front door. Once inside, my shoulder bag, keys, and sunglasses found their place on the entry room table, and I leaned my wrapped package against the wall of the front entrance. Kicking off my sandals as I went, I headed for my favorite overstuffed chair in my living room and sat in a heap, letting myself relax. I sat, looking out my large picture window at the desert vista, thinking about what was to come. I hadn't let my thoughts wander too far, but I knew that this painting would bring back all those memories of that horrific day, memories I thought I had forgotten.

That Arizona day was a stifling hot summer Wednesday in 1967. Many of the homes in Arizona during this time did not have air conditioning. Our home had a swamp cooler. This kind of home climate control is a fairly inexpensive evaporative cooling system that circulates air in homes by running water over cooling pads. Air is blown over these pads and cools the rooms. I mention this because my mom and dad would use any excuse to find a cooler respite from the summer heat of the Arizona desert.

I was twelve years old and the oldest of four children. I usually liked being the oldest, but this year would be different. I always got to do things first because I was "the oldest." At the magic age of thirteen I got to have my ears pierced, while my younger sister had to wait two years for her thirteenth birthday before she could have hers done. I experienced slumber parties, dating, and learning to drive, with my dad as the patient instructor, before the rest of them. Because of this high rank, I thought it gave me the privilege of being able to boss around my younger sisters and brother. They, naturally, didn't see it that way. But, before this day would be over, I would discover that I did not want to be the oldest. I would not want the burden of being the oldest, the one my siblings would turn to in times of trouble.

I knew today was Wednesday because it was my dad's day off. He worked on Saturday, so he got a day off during the week. He worked for a company that served grocery stores with pastries and snack cakes. During the holidays, he sometimes made special runs to stores that ran out of merchandise. His route started from our home in Casa Grande, a small town located between Phoenix and Tucson. He then went to all the surrounding towns, including several trading posts on the Ak-Chin and Gila River Indian reservations.

My parents decided that today we would leave the hot, humidity of our home and escape to one of the local picnic areas at the lake some distance away to the north. Mom started gathering what we needed to take on our day-long outing at the lake: sandwiches, homemade cupcakes, chips, our favorite choice of drink: Kool-Aid, and of course water. Our family never traveled around Arizona without an emergency supply of water, just in case. Most people who live in Arizona for any length of time find out early never to travel without water.

My dad's job in all of this preparation was to make sure our 1962 yellow Comet station wagon was ready for the drive to Canyon Lake. That old car had taken us cross-country from New York state to Arizona four years earlier. After all those miles together, it seemed like part of the family. This was back in the days when wearing seatbelts was not required. My folks would put the backseat down, which extended the seating in the back and enabled me and my sisters, Kate and Terri, and my brother, Jack, to have the whole back of the car to ourselves. We played together with the toys and games we brought along to pass the time during the trip.

This Wednesday morning, the atmosphere in the house was the usual hustle and bustle of getting ready for a picnic. My mother continued to get all the food and other paraphernalia ready. My younger sisters, brother, and I ran around as usual, getting in the way of the preparations while trying to decide what to take with us to keep us occupied on our car trip.

Usually for my sisters and me, it was dolls and books. My brother took his G.I. Joe and a baseball and glove. Today became a special trip because we were going to the lake for our picnic, not just to the city park.

"Hey Rae, can you believe it? We're finally going to the lake. I wonder why Dad changed his mind. I've begged him to take us all summer," Jack said, as he raced around his room gathering up his ball and glove.

"Maybe he agreed because he got tired of you pestering him about it. Jeez, you can be so annoying sometimes." I rolled my eyes at him, but he was too busy to notice as he ran toward the car.

"Rae, come help me please," I heard my mother call from the kitchen. I was in the bedroom I shared with my two sisters. I put down my armload of books and my favorite Barbie doll and headed toward the kitchen.

"Don't touch my stuff," I called over my shoulder to my sister, Kate, as I left the room. She looked up at me in surprise as she started to reach for my new book.

"Rae, put these sandwiches in the ice chest for me, and then mix up the Kool-Aid. Thanks, sweetie. Be sure to fill it with ice first, and don't forget to fill the ice trays."

"Mom," I said exasperated, "I'm not the one who puts the trays back in the freezer empty, remember?"

"Okay, okay, I know. I'm just in a hurry. Your dad is ready to go. Do you kids have all the things ready that you want to take?" she hollered as she stepped around the corner of the kitchen into the hallway, where she found herself asking this question to no one. "Rae, when you're done with the cooler, will you help your sister and brother take everything out to the car? Thanks. I need to finish getting Terri ready."

My mom left the kitchen and I heard her calling for my youngest sister, who was only four years old. I laughed to myself as I pictured the get-up that Terri had dressed herself in this morning. She put on her favorite shirt, one of my brother's which hung well below her knees, no shoes, and a beat up baseball cap that Jack had outgrown. She wouldn't let anyone but my mom help her get dressed.

Much to my chagrin, we never had a swimming pool at our house growing up in Arizona, even though most of our friends did. It seemed like we were the only ones who didn't have one. You see, neither of my parents knew how to swim. In fact, my mother was and still is terrified of the water. Even taking a bath in an overfilled bathtub makes her nervous. A childhood prank nearly caused her to drown. As a young child of eight during a family outing at a lake, her older cousins thought it would be fun to throw her in the water in order to teach her how to swim. Needless to say, it didn't work and she was forever afraid after that to even try to learn. My dad, on the other hand, never developed an interest or the inclination to learn to swim. He grew up in a small town in the rural countryside of New York state where there weren't any public swimming pools. If kids wanted to swim, they went to the creek. It was typically not deep enough to cause him concern, unless it had been a rainy season. He and his dad were avid fishermen, and my grandmother always made sure he had on a life jacket.

All of us kids, however, learned early to swim and spent our summers at the city pool. My two sisters and brother continued to take advanced lessons, and my brother and I took basic life guarding as we got older. However, none of the skills we learned up to that point in our lives could have prepared us for this day, especially when it came to saving adults.

On this day, however, that was the farthest thought from all our minds. Much of our family weekend time together was spent on inexpensive activities such as car tours around the state, picnics, or the drive-in movies, so this particular day didn't seem out of the ordinary.

We were all looking forward to enjoying the water, cooling off, and, as usual, eating our picnic lunch.

It was not until I became an adult that I learned more about the lake and its history. Canyon Lake is a man-made lake, meaning that it had been a canyon in the desert following the natural path of the Salt River, before it was formed by Mormon Flat Dam. The dam was constructed by the Salt River Project in the first half of the 1920s to provide a dependable water supply, as well as water for hydroelectric power. At that time, the recreational area did not have a sandy beach and still doesn't. With a shoreline of more than twenty miles, it is covered with rocky debris and bare desert ground.

The lake itself is not very wide, approximately one mile at its widest point. At times you can hear the sound of boat motors as they speed down the canyon. It is a favorite for slalom skiing in the main bay. The cove where we spread out our picnic, now called Acacia Picnic Site, was about half a mile from the canyon wall, and we could easily see across to the other side. The canyon wall projects into the sky as a solid fortress, giving the place a quiet, secluded feeling. Some ten miles upstream it becomes a restricted passage toward Horse Mesa Dam. It is a serene and mysterious place where boaters can enjoy the quiet solitude and splendor of their surroundings.

The rugged cliffs of this canyon were formed by the up surging of ancient volcanoes. Since then, the Salt River has cut deeply into the convoluted interior of the canyon, forming vertical walls nearly a thousand feet high. Regardless of how treacherous it may seem, this is a truly beautiful canyon. Even today, the only buoys or warning floats on the water tell boaters where the traffic lanes are. At the time of our picnic there were no warning buoys to tell swimmers where water hazards might be.

Remember, we're talking desert here. The water meets the land; there are no waves to wash up fresh sand. It's so rocky you have to wear shoes to protect your feet. In many places there is no sandy bottom to wade in.

Did I tell you that neither of my parents knew how to swim?

When my family arrived at the Canyon Lake Recreational Area, my dad parked the car on the hillside of the road and we walked down the steep side to reach the rocky cove to the picnic area. At the time of our outing, the park service had yet to build a parking lot or ramadas. We found a spot under a mesquite tree and Mom set up our picnic on the desert floor. My sisters, brother, and me ran to the water to enjoy a few minutes of the cool water before being called back when our lunch was ready. We were not the only people there enjoying the day. Even though it was a weekday, the shoreline was scattered with other families enjoying the day same as us. There were several people already swimming and using inner tubes to float with the current of the lake.

One of the other recreational pastimes in this part of the desert is "tubing" the Salt River. Groups of people join friends and tie large inner tubes together and float down the Salt River. Among this flotilla would be a tube designated to hold the styrofoam ice chest. This special ice chest would carry the essential libations for the group. Needless to say, many of the adults tend to become inebriated during their outings, thus making this area particularly dangerous as some have been known to jump off the cliffs for fun, whereby breaking their necks. My parents made it painfully clear during our high school years that, "as long as we were living in their house," we would never be given permission to go tubing. During my high school years this statement became a sore point with me. Much to my displeasure, while many of my high school classmates escaped for senior ditch day, I remained in town to pursue other senior activities that did not involve the Salt River. Even though, by this time, all of us were avid swimmers.

I sat in my comfortable, Mexican, leather chair and chuckled to myself as I remembered those early years. How wise my parents had been. I stood up to stretch and walked to the kitchen to get a glass of iced tea. I came back to the same chair and returned to my musings, my mind still back in 1967.

Mom called to us that lunch was ready and we returned to our picnic spot on shore after splashing and cooling off at the water's edge. We had barely started eating when something caught my dad's eye. Before I realized what was happening, he ran to the water. His sudden motion of leaping up from our picnic spot triggered that sudden prickly sensation of alarm that ran up my arms to the back of my neck. Even though it was a warm day, I felt a chill come over me and looked up at the sky to see if the sun had suddenly gone behind the clouds. My mother and the rest of us sat, rooted on the picnic blanket, looking after him.

I was to find out later that he had seen a small boy, about eight years old, floundering in the water close to shore. The boy was so close to shore, he thought he could reach over and pull him out. At this point, things began to happen very fast. I watched him move toward the water and, before my eyes, my dad took two steps from shore and dropped into the water. He unknowingly stepped off the side of a sheer cliff into a bottomless abyss. He vanished from our sight, as if he was swallowed up by the earth itself.

As I mentioned earlier, Canyon Lake is a deep, desert canyon filled with water. At the time of our picnic, there were no warning markers or buoys to indicate any hazards.

My mother was now acutely alarmed. With shock and horror, we watched our dad disappear beneath the water line as he gasped for air and tried to grab the young boy.

"Rae, stay with them. Don't come near the water!" my mother shouted at me as she ran toward my father. We were instantly on our feet.

By this time my mother was also now at the same point on the shore as my father had been only seconds before. The four of us followed her as far as we dared, forgetting her admonition, and could only stand on shore and scream in terror, not knowing what would happen next. I heard my father yell with a strangled breath to my mother, "Stay there!"

In a huddled, trembling mass we edged a little closer to the water's edge, trying to see my father. My mind was whirling. *I have to do something! I just can't stand here. Oh, God, please help us.*

I stood behind my mother at the edge of the abyss. I was terrified at the thought of what she might do. She stood by us only long enough to hear the start of our screams while watching my father struggle with the young boy. She rushed forward to help, only to fall herself into this unseen and unmarked bottomless pit of water. I have never seen my mother in any more than a shallow bathtub of water. Now she was submerged and out of my sight. "Noooo!" I screamed to my mother, but it was too late. I knew instinctively that she would run to help, but I had been powerless to keep her from jumping in.

Now, both my parents and a child were struggling to free themselves of the drowning waters. I knew that my mother would be helpless in the water. I could no longer see the young boy. Only my dad's head had cleared the water. I found myself at the shore's edge with my younger sisters and brother clinging to me as we screamed for help. My dad was again able to yell to us, "Stay back!"

I knew instinctively that I would never be able to pull them out by myself. All I could think was, *I'm going to lose my parents and I can't do anything to help them. They will drown right before my eyes.* I screamed and cried for help, clinging to my younger sisters and brother.

My dad told me, years later, his thoughts were, "Man, I got to get out of here. I don't know how, but I gotta get out."

At the shore's edge, not only were we witnessing both of our parents facing death, but we were helpless and could only stand, huddled together, panic stricken, while screaming for someone—anyone—to help us.

Somewhere, from the corner of my vision, I saw a flash and felt time slow as we continued to scream and hold one another. Somewhere off shore, a man in an inner tube came running across the cove to where my parents slipped from view. I saw one huge hand reach out, and a voice shouted, "Give me your hand!"

Oh, God. Please help them. My eyes stayed riveted on the head of my father as he once again broke the surface of the water. I had yet to see my mother.

In between cries and sobs, I clutched the small trembling souls of my siblings around me. I had lost track of how long my parents had been fighting the water, but I knew my mother would be suffering the worst kind of fear, if she was still conscious.

My father complied with the stranger's urgent request. He had the boy in a scissor-lock between his legs and my mother by the other hand. Both of them were still under water. Amazingly, all three were pulled out at once and laid on the rocky shore. My attention remained only on my parents' struggle, and not on the stranger who had pulled them out. Would I ever find out who saved our family?

As soon as my parents were pulled from the water, we ran towards them. All three lay sputtering and gasping for breath. The young boy's parents came running down from the roadside where they had been searching for him. No words were spoken at that moment by the young boy's family, only the soft cooing of tender endearments. I watched as the young boy's father picked him up and put him over his shoulder in such a way that water drained from his lungs. I could see from where I stood that he lay like a limp rag, coughing and sputtering over his father's shoulder, spitting out lake water.

My attention was diverted back to my parents, where the young man who rescued them asked, "Are you all right?" He had pulled them from the water as easily as he would a fish on a line. They were shaken but breathing and would recover. I caught my breath long enough to look up into the man's face from across the shimmering heat of the desert landscape. A great feeling of relief washed over me as he looked one last time at us huddled together. He turned away and walked back down the water's edge from where he came.

I could find no words to speak. We were too choked with emotion. We never knew his name or the name of the boy. They vanished from our lives after that dreadful day.

The stranger in our midst disappeared as quickly as he came. Not knowing he had just saved seven lives, for the four of us siblings had nearly become orphans.

When my parents were able to steady themselves, our hysterical screams and crying subsided into whimpers and hiccups. The four of us stood trembling as we realized they were safe once again on shore. We all clung to one another and staggered back to our picnic area. After a few moments passed and we were reassured that they were safe, we began packing our picnic things up. I was trembling so badly from shock and relief that I was barely able to help retrieve our belongings. I glanced at my mother only to find a face I did not recognize. I had never seen the face of death before, but it shook me to my core seeing her that close to dying.

Her usual cheerful face, now white with blue-tinged lips, spoke no words. Her eyes did not register recognition as she looked at me from across the rubble of the desert floor. I took her by the arm and helped her up the steep embankment to our car. Dad carried Terri while she clung to him, hiccupping into his shoulder. Looking back, I saw Kate and Jack holding hands as they helped each other to the car.

No one said a word, no one gave directions, we just simply and quietly began to leave. We had to go home. Our so-called family outing was over. As we began to load the station wagon, Dad put the backseat in place and the three of us older kids sat close together, still too shaken to release our grips on one another. My youngest sister, Terri, was cradled in my mother's arms. They both seemed to need the security of each other's touch. Terri had been too small at the time to truly understand the full impact of what had just happened to our family, but nonetheless was terrified by all of our responses. My mother's face was still pale and her hands shook as she held my youngest sister. I would never know the true terror she experienced that day until many years later. She still, to this day, has difficulty talking about it without tears welling in her eyes.

We rode home in silence. Our day's outing was about fifty miles from home. After about thirty minutes of silence, I was the first one to speak. I do not remember saying this, but as my mother retold this story to me with tears in her eyes, she said, "You spoke up very seriously and said, 'when we get home you have to show me how to use the washer and dryer because if you're not here, I'll have to do it.'"

You see, in my child's mind, being the oldest always made me feel responsible for my sisters and brother. So, I had to know how to run the house in case something happened to my mother and father. At that age, it never occurred to me before that something like death could affect my family.

After I said that, it broke the spell we were all in. The near tragedy of it all was just too much. At this point, my father completely broke down. He slowly pulled the car over and at once we were all crying and hugging. The three of us clamored over into the front seat to be near each other. This was the first time I can remember ever seeing my father cry. I was to experience this overwrought emotion once again years later upon my father's return from his brother's funeral. To witness this overwhelming flood of emotion from a man, especially from my father, left my nerves exposed, as if my skin had been sandblasted. After several long minutes my dad was able to drive again and our tears and sobs slowed. After that, we were able to relax somewhat and talk quietly on the way home.

"You kids listen to me. Your mom and I are alright. We had a bad experience, but we're okay and everything is going to be fine," my dad said to reassure us. My mother was still too shaken to find her voice. All she could do was clutch our sweat-soaked bodies to hers as tears once again rolled down her face.

Jack, Kate, and I climbed over the front seat and sat in the backseat. With a sigh of relief, my brother said, "Boy Dad, you really had me scared. I thought at first you were playing a joke on us, trying to test our swimming skills. When Rae held us back, I knew something was wrong."

My dad looked at us from the rearview mirror and said, "Rae did the right thing. It was too dangerous for you kids to get close. You could have fallen in with us. Even if you thought you could have helped us, none of you were strong enough to pull us all out." Dad reached his arm around to the backseat and patted my brother as a way to reassure him, and the rest of us, that they survived this terrifying afternoon.

"We were very lucky that there was a man close enough to get to us. Did any of you see who he was or where he went?"

"I saw him, Dad, for a minute, just before he started walking down the shore. After we started picking up our things to leave, I turned around to look again, but he was gone," I said, hoping to give him the information he needed.

"Well, thank God he was there when he was," Dad replied as we continued to drive through the mountains heading for home.

I did not find out until many years later that, after this life-changing event, my parents did make some changes. The first being, they made a will stating that in case anything did happen to them, we would be sent to my aunt and uncle in New York state so that we would not become wards of the state. This disturbed me greatly on two levels. Firstly, becoming wards of the state further terrified me because I did not want to be separated from my younger sisters and brother. Secondly, I did not want to go back to New York. I believed that I could take care of my siblings. They also made sure we had certified swimming lessons every summer, to ensure our safety in the water and their peace of mind that we would be as safe as possible around water.

I was not to know what effect this experience had on my parents until many years later. They told me of their discussions with each other about why this happened to their family. Was it to teach them something or prepare them in some way? They could not come to any conclusions other than to show them how important it was to be there for each other. Our family continued to remain close. Even today, we all live in the same city.

What would our lives have been like had my parents perished in that water? I do not care to guess. I do know we continued to grow and thrive as a happy, healthy family. Because we only had each other, our extended family was not there for additional support. We were and continue to remain a close family. If one of us had a concern or a question about this experience over the years, my parents were always available to talk about it. As traumatic as this event was, we never felt that it was something that couldn't be talked about. Today my parents are enjoying their precious grandchildren who, by the way, also know how to swim.

I, of course, was thankful as a child that my parents survived and was glad it was over. I didn't want to think about it again. Ever. Then, thirty years later, I saw the painting hanging in the Scottsdale gallery and all the memories came rushing back.

11

~ *Joe* ~

The Letter

BY EIGHT O'CLOCK, THE morning already began to show signs of another hot day. The sun hung heavy in the clear blue sky and heat waves shimmered off my back patio. I turned on the overhead fan and decided I would enjoy a few more minutes of my second cup of tea while watching the desert wake up. The phone rang just as I settled back and startled me out of my reverie. I walked through the open french doors and reached the phone on the third ring.

"Hello," I said, setting my mug on the cluttered studio table.

"Good morning, Joe. I hope I didn't call too early and disturb you?" Lee said on the other end. I didn't expect to hear from him this early in the day. He didn't usually open the gallery until ten o'clock.

"Good morning, Lee. No problem. I'm an early riser. What's up?" I wondered why he would be calling so early.

"I hate to bother you, especially after our hectic night

at the ArtWalk, but are you, by any chance, coming into town today?"

"Yeah, I'm planning to make a trip in later to pick up some art supplies. I'm getting ready to start on another series of landscapes."

"Good. If you have time, would you be able to stop by the gallery? Rae Warner came in yesterday to pick up your painting. Remember, *Canyon Lake*? She left a letter for you and asked if I would pass it along. I know you're busy. If you don't want it, I can throw it away or send it in the mail. It's up to you."

Oh, Jesus. My mind whirled in confusion. *Why is she doing this?* I didn't realize it, but Lee was talking to me again.

"Joe, are you there? What do you want me to do? She seemed insistent that you get this." Lee's voice sounded a little on edge, and I didn't want him to be imposed upon any further.

"Okay. Listen, I'll stop by on my way to the suppliers. How long are you working at the gallery today? I don't want to keep you waiting." I stalled for time trying to get my thoughts together.

"I'll be here till seven o'clock. If I miss you, I'll drop it in the mail."

"That's fine. Thanks, I'll see you later." By the time I hung up the phone, I decided I would pick up the letter. The more I thought about it, though, the more I doubted my decision. As much as I didn't want to read it, I knew I had to find out if there was any connection between Rae and that day at the lake. It seemed as though I found myself on a downhill path, headed for a collision with my past. Now didn't seem like a good time for me to find out, but I had no choice. Rae had made the choice for both of us.

Later that afternoon, having finished my errands in town and unable to keep delaying the inevitable, I pulled up in front of Lee's gallery. I sat for a long moment in the parking space in front of Lee's large front display window, chastising myself for hesitating. *What's the big deal? Just go in there, get the letter, and be done with it. It's probably only a letter of thanks. Move Joe. Open the Jeep door and walk into the gallery.* I realized my hands felt sweaty even though the air conditioning blew full blast in the Jeep. *Well, buckaroo, let's get this over with,* I said to myself as I took the key out of the ignition and headed toward the gallery.

The bell that Lee has suspended above the door chimed when I entered the cool quietness of the gallery. Lee greeted me as he came out of the workroom. Not only did he display and present artists' work, but he stretched and framed pieces upon request. From the smell of the gallery and his somewhat disheveled appearance, I must have interrupted his work because he came out of the workroom wiping his hands with a soft cloth.

"Looks like you're up to your elbows in work these days."

"Yeah, another six canvases came in today. They want them ready by the end of next week." To most people, this would already cramp a tight schedule. Lee, however, always seemed to make his deadlines.

"Sorry for having to impose on you this way. I hope there won't be any more letters from Ms. Warner," I said. I could feel my brow knit together in a frown.

"Oh, it's no problem. I wouldn't be upset if she came back in, if you know what I mean. I'd like to see more of her," Lee remarked with a quirky grin on his face.

"Yeah, Lee, I'm sure you would. Do you have the letter?" Lee never seemed to have any trouble with women, except that I never saw him with the same one more than a few times. Lee disappeared back into the workroom and came out with an envelope in his hand.

"Sorry about the smudges. I must have left it on one of the work tables and got some solution on it." *Yeah, smudges. It took longer than I thought to loosen the flap. You don't have a chance with her, buddy. She's going to be mine!*

"Thanks for keeping it for me. I'll be in touch with you later, if you want me to come back and pick up any of my paintings I left from the show."

"Not a problem. You can come back anytime, or I can leave them hang here for a while. Just let me know what you want to do," Lee added while he stood in the frame entrance to his workroom.

I turned and walked toward the door. I looked down at the envelope for the first time, turning it from front to back and then to the front again. Yes, I could see faint black smudges on the front and back of it near the flap. My name, written in a neat feminine script with purple ink, appeared slightly smeared. Even though it was sealed at the corners, the center flap was loose. I paused, stopping to look back at Lee, but he had already disappeared back into the workroom. I have known Lee for several years and found him trustworthy in our dealings together. Why would he want to read this letter? I put the letter in my back pocket and headed to the

Jeep. I would have to ask him later about his feelings for Rae.

I drove back toward home with some supplies that I needed for my studio, as well as a few groceries. While I drove, I pulled the envelope from my pocket and glanced at it. It was addressed to me from a woman I briefly met and who has caused me much emotional turmoil over the last few days. I asked myself why, after all these years, the events of this chance meeting happened. I have come to believe that a person may never know why things in our universe happen when and where they do. I don't always understand the reason; I only try to learn to accept it as possible divine intervention and move on. When I got closer to my studio, I decided that, whatever message the letter contained, I would try to help Rae. After all, no one would make up a story like this.

When I pulled into the driveway at the front of the studio, the sun was beginning to slide behind the roofline of the house. The dawn-to-dusk lights I installed for security on the front of the house came on, lighting the entrance. This was my favorite quiet time of the evening, just before the night creatures come out and the daytime fauna have settled into their evening resting places.

When I usually enter the house, the first thing I do is turn on some quiet music, but this evening I didn't. Instead, I sat in front of the large floor-to-ceiling window looking over the desert. The chair lamp that glowed softly over my shoulder was the only light on in the house. Tonight I needed the soft stillness of the desert as I sat in my overstuffed, leather chair to read Rae's letter.

◦—𝕸𝕸𝕸—◦

Dear Mr. Sullivan,

Thank you for accepting this letter and taking the time to read it.

I'm sure my question to you earlier was quite a shock and somewhat confusing. But I had such a strong feeling about your painting when I saw it and, judging by your reaction, I had to ask.

I would still like very much to talk with you about your work and how you came to choose the site of Canyon Lake to paint. You see, this area has a very special meaning for my family and me.

If you have some free time, please call me. Your friend, Lee has my number.

Sincerely,
Rae Warner

P.S. I hope you don't mind me saying, but you have the most amazing blue eyes. I noticed them at the ArtWalk that night. For a moment, I thought I had seem them somewhere before.

◦—𝕸𝕸𝕸—◦

I sat for several minutes, just holding the letter in my hand, and then reread it. What did she mean about my eyes? I decided I would call Lee in the morning and get her phone number. I reminded myself about my earlier conversation and regretted my abruptness with her. I could at least talk to her on the phone and apologize.

The next morning, after my customary breakfast of tea, fruit, and toast, I called Lee. I made my call after ten o'clock, but he didn't pick up so I left a message on his machine asking for Rae Warner's phone number. This gave me some time to decide whether or not I was making the right decision. Maybe I could quickly and easily answer her questions and be done with it. Her request sounded simple enough. *Don't sweat it,* I told myself.

I made use of the time and also kept my mind off of what happened years ago by getting my sketches and canvases ready. I had scheduled a lot of work for myself in the coming months and I didn't need any distractions along the way.

～※※※～

Lee made his way up the steps from the gallery's basement vault when he heard his answering machine click off. He thought he had heard a voice, but couldn't make out what the caller said. He stepped over to his desk and saw a flashing red light. He pushed the message button as he laid down the rest of the framing tools. The familiar voice of Joe Sullivan was asking for Rae Warner's phone number.

"Damn," he said aloud. No one was in the gallery at the time. It was still too early for most of the regular patrons to be out. He listened to the message and said, to no one but himself, "What the hell does this mean? I thought you weren't interested, buddy."

Lee turned from the desk and went back into the workroom. "I'll give it to you when I'm damn good and ready," he said, looking back over his shoulder at the phone number written in red on his desk pad.

～※※※～

Later that day the phone rang as Joe had finished sketching his basic drawing on a new canvas.

"Hello."

"Hey, Joe, this is Lee. I got your message. Sorry I

didn't get back to you sooner, but I've had people in here off and on all afternoon."

"That's okay. I've been busy here trying to get started on that commission job. I just wanted to get Rae's phone number. She said she left it with you. She still has some questions about the painting. I thought I'd give her a call."

"Yeah, I've got it here somewhere, hang on," he replied with a little too much disgust in his voice.

I could hear Lee set the phone down as he shuffled papers on his desk. When he picked up the phone again, I heard the bell on the gallery door chime in the background.

"Here it is. Are you ready? It's 555-1758. I thought you weren't interested in talking to her, you change your mind?"

"Well, not exactly. Maybe I can answer her questions and be done with it."

"Good luck, Joe. I gotta run. Someone just came in. Let me know how it goes." With that, Lee hung up and I stood in my studio holding the phone, staring at it. *Lee didn't sound at all like himself. Maybe he's starting to feel the stress of running the gallery all by himself.*

I paced around the studio with Rae's phone number in my hand. *No time like the present,* I said to myself. All this indecision and thinking about the past has interfered enough.

As I dialed the number, I looked at the clock. It was after four, maybe she wouldn't be home and I could just leave a message.

"Hello," a soft voice said. *Oh, God. I should hang up*

now. My hand would not move and my voice stuck in my throat.

"Hello, is anyone there?"

"Oh, yes. Ms. Warner? This is Joe Sullivan. Is this a good time to call? I hope I'm not disturbing you?" This all came out too fast. *Take a breath and slow down*, I told myself.

"Please, call me Rae. No, you're not disturbing me. In fact, I was just trying to decide on where to hang my new painting."

"I received the letter you left for me with Lee. Rae, I apologize for being so short with you the other night at the gallery. What questions can I help answer for you?" I found it difficult to swallow. My mouth had no moisture.

"Thank you, Mr. Sullivan, for calling me. I'm sure you must be very busy." The voice on the other end sounded sincere and much calmer than my own.

"Rae, please call me Joe."

"Thank you, Joe. Well, when I was in Lee's gallery and saw your painting, I just couldn't help but stare at it. The oddest sensation came over me, and all of a sudden I remembered a tragic experience I had at the lake when I was a child. It all became so real to me as I stood there and looked at it. I'm sure this doesn't make any sense to you at all."

My heart began to thud against my chest, making it difficult for me to breath. I covered the mouthpiece of the phone with my hand and swung it away from my face. I inhaled deeply and let it out through my mouth. When I recovered my breath, I returned the phone to my ear.

"Rae, I think we should meet. This all makes perfect sense. Can you meet me at Lee's gallery tomorrow afternoon at one o'clock?" For the first time in a week, I felt a relieved calmness. There was a long pause on the other end of the line and I thought she might have hung up. "Rae, are you there?"

"Yes, Joe. I'm here. What did you mean that this all makes perfect sense?"

"Rae." *Oh, God. How was I going to say this?* "I was at the lake that day. I was the one who pulled your parents out of the water."

12

The Calm Before the Storm

I COULDN'T BELIEVE WHAT I just heard. When the phone rang, I answered it, standing in my kitchen. Now, hearing these astonishing words, suddenly my legs were unable to support me and I slid down against the wall and sat on the floor.

Finding my voice, barely a whisper, I choked out, "Joe, it was you? Did you just say that you were the one who saved my parents?"

Joe confirmed what I had heard, saying, "Yes, Rae. It was me."

I don't remember what I said next, but I do remember agreeing to meet Joe the following day at the gallery, and then hung up the phone. I went to the sink for a glass of water and went into the living room and sat down in the closest chair and stared out the picture window at the desert sunset. I couldn't believe it. After all these years, this might be the chance for me to have those long ago questions answered. Even though I began to feel uneasy about the possible outcome, I knew I had to meet Joe Sullivan. My attention was once again drawn to the rough-hewed, wooden frame of the painting sitting on the floor, waiting to be hung.

While I sat in the quiet of my living room with the doors and windows open, I felt the light touch of a breeze waft through the room. I could smell the desert air as it rustled the palo verde tree in the courtyard. The soft stirring of the air drew my attention to the clouds that began to form from the southeast. The monsoon season was here and evening storms were common. The dark sky looked like it would bring rain. I walked into the courtyard and stood, bathing myself in moon glow. Lifting my face upward with my eyes closed, I could smell the rain on the air. *Was the time finally right for me to find my answers? I need to know if he's the one that can tell me.*

⚬━⁓

Joe's sleep that night was disturbed, to say the least. He was totally off guard by his sudden admission to Rae. He knew that it was quite a shock for her as well, based on her reaction. His dreams were filled with rushing water and screaming children. What would he say to her tomorrow?

When he pulled up to the gallery the next afternoon, Lee stood out front with a broom in his hand. Joe could tell by the look on his face he was not happy. A slight frown replaced his usual cocky smile. He was not there to sweep his front sidewalk. Lee wanted to be sure to see Joe when he arrived.

When Lee saw Joe pull into the parking space in front, he opened the car door. "Lee, I'm sorry I didn't call you to let you know what was going on. I decided to meet Rae here. It seemed like the best place. I hope you don't mind."

"Well, are you going to tell me what's going on? Rae's already here. She's been waiting for ten minutes." Lee followed Joe into the gallery as he walked quickly to the entrance.

"I'll tell you all about it later. Can you give us a few minutes alone?" He looked at Lee with what must have been a disturbing expression because Lee opened the office for them with no further questions.

Yes, Joe thought, as Rae turned to face them when the door chime announced their arrival. She was the same small, petite woman he had seen at the gallery opening the other night. Her slightly disheveled blonde hair, held up with a wooden pick, highlighted a youthful face for a woman close to forty. Joe could see, by the light coming in through the windows, that her lips were tinted with shades of faded lipstick. She looked as though she got as much sleep as he did last night.

They stood facing each other, searching for some trace of recognition from all those years ago. Frowning at the same time, they found none. Joe saw Rae give off a slight shiver as he stepped forward to take her outstretched hand.

"Rae, hello, I'm Joe. I'm pleased to meet you," he said as he searched her face, for what he wasn't sure. Joe had hoped she would somehow make this easier for him. He felt a slight tingling sensation run up his arm as their hands clasped one another. Her hand felt warm and gripped his with strong self-assurance even though her face reflected a different emotion of strain and hopefulness.

"Hello, Joe. This is all so sudden, forgive me for . . ." her voice trailed off and she ducked her head, trying to hide the deep emotions that had overcome her and drained her face of color.

"No need to apologize, I understand. This is quite a shock for me as well. Would you like some water?"

~~~

I finally gathered my wits and looked at the man who stood in front of me. Up close, he looked younger than I thought he would because of his calm demeanor and tall, trim physique. He wore his thick, black hair collar-length. Threads of gray streaked his hair, slightly tousled from his apparent rush to the gallery. His face revealed the same distraught emotion I felt. The dominant blue-gray eyes I noticed earlier seemed to search my face. I felt a shiver as I reached behind myself for the nearest chair and sat down. I fumbled for the glass of water Lee had given me earlier and nearly spilled it as I drained it.

~~~

"Rae, if you feel up to it, I would like you to see my studio and we could continue our talk in private. My studio is at the base of the Superstition Mountains off Highway 88. If you can follow me through traffic, it will be a short drive from the highway turnoff up the mountain."

I can't believe I said this. Joe, get hold of yourself. Hopefully she won't accept and we can stay here.

"Yes, I think that would be a good idea. I have my car, I can follow you." *I must be out of my mind with de-*

lusion. Why did I say yes? Rae, breathe. Take a breath and breathe, for God's sake.

As we made our way out of the gallery, we said our goodbyes to Lee and apologized for taking up his time. After a few more minutes of gathering my thoughts, I found myself behind the wheel of my car, following a late model Jeep, driven by a man who filled me with more questions than answers. Yes, he was rather good looking in an artistic sort of way. No matter how ridiculous this sounded, and as crazy as I knew this little adventure was, I could not stop the car and turn it around.

After all these years, I found myself on a journey, and I wasn't sure I was ready for it. Too many things were already falling into place for me to stop now. First, finding the painting. Then, Joe saying that he was at the lake that day. It was too incredible to believe. Maybe I was going off in a totally wrong direction, but I had to find out. I had to know; my family had to know. So I kept driving, following a Jeep that did its best not to lose me in traffic. I knew I couldn't get lost; I could always find my way home. I knew what direction he headed when he told me his studio was at the base of the Superstition Mountains.

The irony of all this kept my foot on the gas; my own home was in sight of another set of mountains to the southwest. The San Tan Mountains may not be as majestic as the Superstitions, but none the less beautiful.

While Joe drove through town, leading the way with

Rae behind him, his thoughts were mangled with self-doubt. He couldn't believe she agreed to follow him. What was he going to do when they got to the studio? What if this is some kind of joke? What if it's not? What if she was there? She can't be part of this; too much time has passed. Why did he drive that day to Tortilla Flats and stop at the canyon to paint that picture? Maybe . . . he did it for her . . . *Oh, this is just too crazy.*

Joe didn't even remember driving through all the traffic. He did remember keeping his eyes glued to the rear view mirror, going slow enough to keep her behind him. They made it safely to the east valley and turned off Highway 88, headed toward the studio. *Oh God, what kind of shape did I leave the studio in? I left without giving it a second thought. I had no plans at the time to bring anyone here. Hell, why do I care—she isn't going to stay. But . . . I do care, for some strange reason.*

⸙

I pulled up behind him in front of a large adobe home with natural desert landscaping. I breathed a sigh of relief when I recognized my surroundings. I began to relax, knowing I could leave easily and without difficulty. I needed to make sure to leave before it got too dark.

This area seemed to be void of city amenities, such as streetlights and sidewalks.

I noticed all of this while I waited in my parked car behind the Jeep. Joe slowly made his way out of his own vehicle. I remained seated in the car, making a last minute decision to stay and give myself a few more minutes to calm the pounding in my chest. I watched him leave his vehicle and walk slowly to the driver's side of my car, looking in the windshield as he came close, as if to make sure I was still there. A smile seemed to start across his face, and then quickly disappeared as he approached my door.

I had my window down and, surprisingly, he put both hands on the frame and bent down to ask me if I wanted to still see the studio. Although I wasn't sure, I said yes as best as my voice would permit. I suddenly found all the moisture in my mouth gone and my tongue refused to cooperate.

When he opened the car door for me, I reached for the door absentmindedly and brushed his hand. A sudden shock ran through me, making the hair on my arm stand up. It must have come from the static electricity in the air on this humid summer afternoon. Monsoon storms were prevalent this time of year. I followed him from the gravel drive into a tile patio with a lattice covered awning. I noticed the temperature was immediately cooler. An outdoor fountain with its soft, bubbling water added to the overall tranquil feel of this quiet repose.

My earlier uneasiness began to fade and I flexed my shoulders as he guided me to an old, leather Mexican-style chair. He asked if I would wait here while he got us something cool to drink. I willingly agreed, as this would give me a few moments to gather my thoughts. If nothing else, his home and studio was a peaceful place and he appeared to want to make me as comfortable as possible. I began to wonder just what I might learn about Joe Sullivan, the artist, before this day came to an end. I suddenly became anxious to learn his motivation about painting that picture. Why Canyon Lake of all places?

When Joe opened Rae's door to help her out of the car, his hand brushed against hers and he felt that faint buzz again. They both looked up at the same time. Did she feel that? It must be his imagination. He wanted to get her to the patio and inside the house as quickly as possible and sit her down. He hoped to escape to the kitchen for a few minutes to think about what he was going to say while he got them something to drink.

Returning with the drinks, he noticed her face looked much calmer and a faint smile spread on her face as he sat across from her.

"What a peaceful place you have here, Joe. It must be a great place to create," she said as she looked around the room. Her attention paused here and there, but rested on the large window facing the mountainscape on the backside of his house.

"Yes, I enjoy it very much. Painting and creating music here comes easily. I moved to Arizona when I was a kid and never wanted to leave. I bought this house several years ago from a friend of my sister's and spend most of my time here, when I'm not traveling." He sat back in his chair to catch his breath. He realized he was talking too fast. "I'm sorry, I'm babbling. Tell me how you happened to come into Lee's gallery that night at the ArtWalk?"

A nervous smile began to spread over her face and she suddenly began looking everywhere, except at him.

Joe thought he detected a slight flushing at the tips of her ears.

When her eyes came back to his face, her gaze focused directly at his eyes. Joe suddenly felt that buzz again, even though she sat across from him. He repositioned himself in his chair, as if to give her more room and guard himself against the coming answer.

"Oh, well, it was quite by accident. I have lived in the valley myself for quite a long time, but had never gone to the Scottsdale ArtWalk before. I found myself with some free time that evening and asked a friend to go with me. He's someone I work with and have known a long time, so we sometimes go places together."

"So, you're not married?" Realizing what he had asked her, he felt a deep flush creep up his face.

She looked at him again and her smile grew to where he could now see a shiny, white row of perfect teeth.

"No, I'm not married. I was . . . once, but that was a long time ago. Anyway, we were walking in and out of the galleries. I really had no intentions of buying anything. I wanted to see some of the different pieces of art and get out and do something that night."

"Well, for whatever reason, it was quite serendipitous that you did. Would you like to see the studio now?" She nodded her head and moved her chair back as she stood. The leg of her chair snagged on one of the tile edges. Joe reached over and helped pull the chair away. Her shoulder brushed against his arm as she moved in front of him. He could smell the faint trace of her perfume. It was something clean and fresh that made him close his eyes and take another breath. He walked ahead of her to show her into the main part of his house and down the hallway to the studio that occupied the east side.

It was late afternoon by the time they got back to the mountain and the sun was positioned to the west side of the house. The studio still had enough natural light, but it was subdued with a feeling of serenity about it. Anyone who walked into the room was immediately drawn to the wall-sized window that looked out over the desert.

At this time of day, the mountain's colors were lit by the fading sun. For Joe, this was one of the best times to paint. He found himself frequently sitting out on his patio, playing his guitar as the sun sank lower. He enjoyed watching some of his desert neighbors, such as rabbits, lizards, and quail, searching for their evening meal. He found himself thinking, without realizing it, about how glad he was at that moment that someone was there to share this beautiful place with him.

Rae stood in front of the window and stared wide-eyed at the scene before her. Her words came out soft, as if she were talking to herself.

"I will never get over the beauty of this place." Joe moved to her side and felt himself thinking the same thing. Shortly, they came out of their silent reverie and Joe moved around the studio, picking up and replacing things, as if to straighten up the clutter. It would do no good; it would look the same after a few days anyway, he thought. He had several canvases stacked along one wall, ready to use, and two easels standing with half-done paintings on them. Over the years, his work habits were sporadic at best. He put himself under additional pressure by having several projects going at once. One side of the studio was wall-to-wall storage cabinets. Some of the doors remained open and he walked along next to the counter tops and closed them as he picked up brushes, paint tubes, and other miscellaneous accouterments of his trade. He felt nervous for some reason and wanted to keep his hands busy. Very few people had ever been in his studio. Lee had not even seen his place. He had always been generous about letting him bring work in that people requested so they could see it hung on a wall with perfect lighting.

Joe's attention shifted back to Rae. As he watched her from the corner of his eye, he found her standing at the window. He turned to watch her as she moved from one side of the window to another. She had a quiet beauty about her. She paused now and then as she moved deftly from one end to the other without bumping into the small stool and electrical cords that he used for his sound system, which were strung across the floor. Her back was straight and she tilted her head, first one way, then another to get a better angle of whatever it was that caught her attention outside. Her slender hips swayed gently as she made her way across the floor. She turned her frame toward him and he met her calm, upturned, smiling face. It took several moments before he realized she had spoken to him.

As Rae turned from the scene in front of her and looked at Joe with penetrating blue eyes, she asked, "Tell me about that day. Tell me what you remember. Please . . . if you can, I need to know."

"Rae, I'm sorry. I understand your need to know,

but this is very difficult for me. It's been years since I thought about this. I don't know if I can talk about it. You see." He paused and tried to stop the feeling that his heart was going to jump out of his chest. Rae remained where she was and waited silently for Joe to continue. He started again.

"You see . . . when I was about the same age as when you had your experience, I was with my family at a lake. Actually, at the time, my mother had remarried and I was with her and my younger sister and my stepfather. Anyway, we spent the day water skiing and swimming. There was an accident and something happened to my stepfather. I found out later that he had a heart attack and drowned. I was there Rae. I watched it happen and I couldn't help him. The guilt just about killed me." He paused and tried to recover from the dizziness he felt.

"So, you see, when I was at Canyon Lake with my friends all those years ago and I saw it about to happen again to you and your family, I knew I had a chance to do something this time." He walked toward her and found himself standing in front of the window, looking at the mountain in front of him. "I was there, Rae, for a reason. I believe that now, to help you . . . and to help myself."

Now his hands began to shake. Rae moved closer and stood beside him, looking up into his face, and noticed the paleness that spread over him. She rested her hands lightly on his. They were soft and warm. Joe turned to look in her distraught face and saw tears welling in her eyes. His hands stopped shaking and he put his arms around her. He could hear soft, little sobs come from her as she clung to him. He pressed his face against her hair and once again breathed in her soft scent. He felt his body relax as he held her until she looked up at him with a smile on her face.

13

The Evidence

THEY STOOD TOGETHER FOR what seemed like an eternity. Joe's heart beat so fast, he knew Rae must have felt it too. He tried to regain some composure, standing with his feet apart, supporting Rae as she sobbed into his chest. He held onto her until she caught her breath and took a step away from him. He led her to the sofa and they sat side-by-side until she reached for her drink. Her face searched his for answers.

"Rae, are you okay for a minute?" She nodded silently, dabbing a tissue against her eyes. "I have something I want to show you. I'll be right back."

Joe left Rae sitting there while he went to his bedroom and opened his closet. He knew what he was looking for, but he hadn't seen it in years. He remembered finding the box again when he had moved into this house, and had almost thrown it out. Now he understood the reason for keeping it.

On the top shelf, way in the back, sat an old shoe box patiently waiting for them to discover its meaning. Joe pulled it free from the other miscellaneous debris he had collected over the years. His mind flooded with memories, as scenes from that day came back to him.

⌒〰〰〰⌒

When Joe left the room, I got up and tried to walk around.

My legs felt like I'd run a marathon and I quickly sat back down. My hands trembled slightly and I felt my breathing come back to normal after my uncontrolled sobs subsided. I felt dizzy with the sudden possibilities. *After all these years, I hoped to find my answers.*

Joe came back into the room carrying a tattered, old shoebox. He sat down next to me with the box perched on his lap, like it might explode any minute.

⌒〰〰〰⌒

"Rae, I've had these for years and several times came close to throwing them out. I wasn't sure why I kept them, but now I think I know why. Maybe now you can answer some questions for me."

When he lifted the lid, Rae leaned in closer to him, not only to see better, but that he might give her some protection against what lay in the box. When he pulled the lid away, Rae let out a soft gasp. Her hands reached forward to touch the old moccasins inside, just to make sure they were real. She looked up at Joe with a face so drained of color he thought she might faint.

"Where did you get these?" she asked as her voice shook.

Before Joe could answer, Rae lifted out the shoes, stiff from age and water. They were dark brown, rough leather with a once thick and plush sheep skin lining what was now flat. Flecks of dirt and twigs still clung to the inside. Rae plucked a small piece of driftwood from the inside of the shoe and asked again, "Where did you get these? Did they come from the lake?"

All Joe could say was, "Yes."

Rae searched his face desperately for answers. "Tell me, please, Joe," she asked with a pleading in her voice.

"Yes," Joe said again, this time swallowing the hard lump in his throat.

"I found them after I pulled those people, your parents, out of the water. They must have reached the surface after all the commotion, when the water subsided. I saw them bob to the surface and reached down to pick them out of the water. I started to ask the man if they were his, but he was already huddled around the children and woman way up away from the shoreline." Joe realized this all came out in one breath and he paused a moment before he continued.

"I guess I was in a bit of shock myself, so I just turned around and walked back down the shoreline to find my buddies."

Rae continued to look at him in disbelief. When she finally found her voice, she said, "Those were my father's shoes. He lost them when he went into the water. Oh, my God. Joe, I can't believe this."

"Rae, tell me what happened that day," Joe pleaded.

⚡︎

I looked in the shoebox and saw the old leather moccasins. I knew whose they were and where they came from. I am sure by the recognition on my face that Joe knew they meant something to me. I knew he wanted an explanation after he told me how he came to find them.

Everything came back in a roar, making my head throb. I sat back against the sofa for support, with my hands on my face, and tried to think how I was going to start telling him all that had happened. I don't know how long we sat there side by side, but as I poured out the events of that day, Joe sat close and held my hand. When I finished relating the horror of the day, I felt limp from exertion. Joe put his arm around me and pulled me close. He allowed me time to settle my thoughts until I was ready to go on.

I looked up at him and said, "You have no idea what you did that day. You not only saved the lives of the three people you pulled out of the water, but you saved the lives of those four children, me and my sisters and brother. Our lives would have been forever changed if you had not done what you did."

⌐═❀❀❀═⌐

While Rae continued her story, Joe sat there speechles. He couldn't have interrupted her if he wanted to. He had no voice because of the large lump in his throat. He was reliving the terror of that day along with her.

Rae paused, taking a deep breath and continued. "We have often wondered who the man was that saved us. My father wanted to talk to him and thank him for what he did, but the man disappeared by the time we started gathering up all our things."

The lump in his throat had finally been swallowed and he said, "I know. I hesitated for only a short time and then started walking back down the shoreline. I remember, at the time, being too stunned to do much else. It wasn't until years later, when I came to Canyon Lake again and started the painting, that it all came back to me. I don't know why, but that painting was sketched in one day and I finished painting it in a week. I have never completed a piece that quickly before. Rae, I realize now that I did it for you . . . and me." He paused for a breath. "I am glad you found it," he told her as he reached to brush away a tear that had escaped from her red, swollen eyes and rolled down her face.

Rae had been listening closely and never took her eyes away from his face, as if she was looking for a flicker of deceit. She never found any, and, with a sigh of relief, she came out of her trance-like state and shook off the effects.

They both sat back in silence and sipped their drinks, once cool with ice, now warm and tasteless. Joe started to retrieve fresh ones, but Rae caught him by the arm and he sat back down. She turned toward him and drew her legs up underneath her. She sat quietly for a moment and Joe saw her brows come together in concentration. She drew his hands into hers and studied them with interest. She ran her hands along each finger. Turning his hand over, she now studied the palms and wrists. Her hands were warm and Joe felt that faint vibration he had felt earlier, as she ran her hands from his fingertips to his wrist.

⚬─────

His hands . . . I noticed them briefly at the gallery, but now, as I held them in mine, I began to look at them more closely. Joe sat there inert, probably afraid to break the spell. But he didn't draw back as I continued my investigation.

They were not the hands of a man who used them for tools as hard labor; they were used as the tools to express the gift of his soul. His fingers were long, not exactly thin, but contained well-developed muscles and smooth joints. His nail beds were smooth and even with no trace of paint. As I held them up to my face and brushed them across my lips, I did notice a faint smell of hand cleaner that he must use to clean up with. He did not have any noticeable scars or unusual markings on either hand. He wore no rings. His knuckles were slightly creased and hairless. They were the kind of strong hands that would render you helpless if given a massage. I closed my eyes and envisioned them running along my back and neck. I lifted one hand again and gently ran it across my face, feeling the roughness and softness come together as a finger reached out and once again touched my lips. When I opened my eyes, Joe's eyes remained closed and he was breathing shallowly through his nose.

14

The Fated

RAE SEEMED TO TEMPORARILY regain her composure and pulled Joe back to sit beside her. He felt a tremor, a slight flush of heat, as she turned toward him. *Is this rush from her or from me?* he wondered. He could not decide; too many thoughts began to course through his brain at this point. He settled back and tried to calm his racing heart.

She held his hands in hers and examined them closely, for what he didn't know, but he found himself totally helpless. Small vibrations started in his hands from his fingertips to his wrists and up his arms, making the hair stand up as she ran her hands over his. He couldn't help but close his eyes and sit very still. He was afraid to move for fear she would vanish like a dream before his eyes.

He'd never had a professional massage, but the sensations he felt were somewhere between total relaxation and a sexual excitement he had not felt in a long time. He didn't quite understand why these sensations overcame him the way they did, but he was afraid to take a breath or move for fear of breaking this bit of magic that the woman before him seemed to have over him.

Joe had, by now, lost all track of time. He knew that the sun had long since set and the quiet stillness of the desert began to make its way into the house. The sound of distant cicadas and crickets flowed in through the open windows on a waft of air from the patio. She must have sensed some subtle change as well because she looked up at him to ask a question, which brought him rushing back to the present.

"You know what this means, don't you?" she asked.

Joe came slowly out of his reverie when she stopped her ministrations and held his hands in hers. It took him a moment to realize she had spoken.

"No," he said with little breath left. "What does it mean?"

He didn't want to hear her answer, afraid of what she would say and vanish like a fleeting wrath.

"Joe," she paused, taking a deep breath, "us finding each other like this, me being drawn to your painting after all these years and finding it. We were supposed to find each other." She sat back and took another breath.

"What do you think? What are you feeling?" She wanted to know.

"Rae, I don't know what to think. I honestly don't. The last few days have been pretty amazing for me." He turned toward her and pulled her closer. He took a deep breath and spoke slowly. "Rae, I don't want you to go tonight, I want you to stay with me. Besides, it's too dark for you to go back down the mountain alone at this time of night. We have too much to talk about."

He hadn't thought about this before he said it, it just all came out before he had a chance to think about it. Rae got up and walked toward the open window. He sat watching her, wondering what she was thinking and what she might do next.

This is happening too fast, Joe thought to himself. *I need some time to sort out my thoughts, but at the same time, I don't want her out of my sight. What I've come to feel, I cannot deny. I feel as if I have just stepped off a merry-go-round.*

⸙

I stood up and walked to the open window. I suddenly needed some fresh air and was surprised to look through Joe's window and find total darkness. I had planned to leave much earlier, but now . . .

"You're right; it is too dark to go alone. Would you mind letting me follow you down to the highway? I really would like to stay, but I think I should go for now. We both have a lot to think about."

Joe must have had a look of dejection on his face, because as he moved to the window next to her, she quickly said, "Joe, I feel the same. I want to be with you, but I need some time to absorb all this."

"Yes, I know. I understand. It's all been unbelievable for me, too. You're right. I'll take you as far as the highway. Can I call you tomorrow?"

"I would be disappointed if you didn't. I'll be ready to talk with you again by then."

They began walking slowly, shoulder-to-shoulder, toward the back of the house and out to the driveway.

"Thank you, Joe, for sharing everything with me. My family won't believe this, especially these." She held up the shoebox with the old shoes that would be returned to her father.

"I'm glad I kept them for you." Joe opened the car door and moved toward her, wanting to touch her again to make sure all this had really happened. She leaned into him and put her arms around him.

For a moment, they stood wrapped in each other's arms, while a distant coyote called for its mate, adding timbre to the quiet solitude of the desert. A full moon glowed bright overhead with a dark blue velvet sky providing a backdrop, as if it were a curtain closing on an unforgettable play.

15

The Refusal

LEE ARRIVED AT THE gallery earlier than normal because he wanted to make sure everything was in place for his visitor. Ever since the night of the ArtWalk, when he first saw Rae, he knew those old feelings would be coming back to him.

No one in his close circle of friends knew why he really left Denver and moved his business to Scottsdale. He wanted to keep it that way. After his wife recovered from his last assault, she made sure he would never find her again. Divorce papers were filed and signed without him ever seeing her again. He hired a private detective to track her down, but she hadn't been found yet. He thought he could make a fresh start and put his obsessions behind him. The judge ordered him to get therapy and said that if he was ever arrested again he would face prison time for assault.

Lee didn't care about any of that now. How could he, with what he had in mind? All he could think about was Rae. He needed to plan this carefully if it was going to work. His meeting Rae Warner became the final piece he needed to make his biggest deal come together. With her looks and his knowledge of the art world, they would make a great team. *Hell, when I get a few more things in place, my international connections will be under way. My clients don't even know what's going on right under their noses. As long as they are paid their asking price, what does it matter what I charge potential buyers?*

Lee picked up the phone and began dialing Rae's number. *It is eight o'clock. She'd better be home.* He counted each ring, hoping he would not have to listen to the answering machine. On the third ring, she picked up.

"Hello," Rae answered her phone as she stepped out of the shower, still dripping and trying not to slip on the floor.

"Hi Rae, this is Lee from the gallery. I hope I didn't call at a bad time."

"Oh, hi, well, I just got out of the shower. Sorry, hang on a minute, will you?"

Lee could hear the phone crash to the floor and a door shut. While he waited for Rae to return, he envisioned her wet, slick body as she stepped out of the shower. That long hair sticking to her breasts and down her back. He was going to enjoy having her around. His heart began to beat faster and his breath caught in his throat when Rae came back to the phone.

"Okay, I'm back. Oh, before I forget, thanks for passing my letter on to Joe for me. I really appreciate it."

"Sure, no problem, glad I could help." *Damn, why did she have to bring him up?* "I was calling to see if you might be free today? I just received some special order pieces from another local dealer that I thought you might be interested in and then we could grab some lunch."

"It's nice of you to think of me Lee, but I really can't

today. I have a full day planned. Maybe we could do it another time. Would you mind?"

"Well, I know it's short notice, but I will only have these pieces for a short time. Is there any way you can come by later?" *I hate it when they make me beg.*

"I'm sorry Lee, I really can't. I've already made plans to visit my parents. Can I come in tomorrow?"

Something in Lee's voice sounded a little off. It was as if there was some underlying desire he couldn't quite conceal. Even though Rae couldn't place it, a feeling of apprehension crept into the pit of her stomach. She shook it off, dismissing it as paranoia.

"Yeah, okay. Just make sure it's tomorrow. Goodbye, Rae."

"Bye, Lee."

He carefully placed the receiver on the cradle and stood, staring out the front window of the gallery. "You're damn right, it better be tomorrow. What's one more day? It will give me some extra time making sure everything is ready," he said to no one but himself.

Lee busied himself for the next few hours, going over the arrangements he made, making sure the shipping information was set for the canvases to be sent to Europe. He made sure his passport was ready and had a fake one made for Rae after she bought *Canyon Lake* with her credit card. All he needed was her picture. He planned to get that the next time he saw her. An old friend owed him a favor and he was able to get the rest of the information off the internet.

16

The Visit

IT SEEMED LIKE YEARS since Joe last talked with Lee. Lee called as he finished his second cup of morning tea. Joe was sitting out back, listening to the desert wake up and smelling the creosote bushes, as a family of quail scurried across the yard. A covey of mourning doves were cooing from his canopy-limbed mesquite tree when the phone rang.

"Hey, buddy, how are you doing? I thought I'd call and ask if you'd like to come in and go over the receipts of your show. We had an amazing night." Lee's voice sounded excited and full of energy. Joe was surprised, especially after the long weeks of late night preparations and all the extra promotion he put into it.

"Yeah, I'm glad to hear it. Would you mind if I came by sometime next week? I am working on another project right now. This new commission assignment has got me all tied up. This is the first time I'm working with a deadline. Can you send me what I need to sign and I'll get with you on the rest later? I'm sorry, Lee. I'm sure this is an inconvenience for you, but I'd really appreciate it if you would just drop the papers in the mail."

Joe hoped it didn't sound like he was putting Lee off, but he needed some time to recover from the last few days, in addition to keeping up with his increasing workload.

"Okay," Lee said, trying to keep the disappointment out of his voice. "How about I call you later? Oh, by the way, how did the meeting go with Rae?" He waited patiently for Joe's response.

Joe had hoped Lee would have forgotten about the little episode that took place in his gallery. With the closing of his show and hanging a new series of artwork, he would have preferred it to slip his mind, but he knew Lee would ask him eventually. Nothing ever got past Lee's critical eye. He had been there to see Joe's reaction to Rae's letter, as well as his speedy arrival to take her out of the gallery as soon as possible.

"Oh, we had an interesting conversation. Yes, she's familiar with the area around Canyon Lake. I'll tell you about it sometime. Thanks for letting me know about wrapping up the show. I'll get back to you soon. Thanks, Lee."

Lee couldn't believe it. *What the hell is going on?* He paced back and forth around his desk, trying to work this out in his head. *Were these two seeing each other? Why couldn't Joe just stay out of this? If they are together, this is going to complicate things. Or is it . . . ?*

━━✎━━

Well, so much for my morning peace and quiet. Joe put away the phone and headed toward the kitchen to dump his remaining cold tea into the sink. *What happens next?* Looking at the ticking clock hung on the wall, it was still too early to call Rae. After they exchanged phone numbers last night, he found himself hoping she would call him first. He moved from room to room, pacing like a teenager waiting for the phone call that would never come. *God, what would I say to her? I probably said too much last night; she may never want to see me again, let alone talk to me.* He knew he wanted to see her again. He needed to. There were still too many unanswered questions. Being around her somehow made him realize what he had been missing all these years. *Maybe she's the one who can help me get peace back into my life. Our lives,* he thought. He was beginning to think that her life was in as much turmoil as his because of their past experiences. This whole unbelievable coincidence was overwhelming.

Joe was in the studio, looking out the large window again, staring at the endless beauty of the desert. When finding himself in this kind of mental turbulence, he normally picks up his guitar or sketchpad and waits for the stress or emotional strain to come out. Doing something with his hands has always helped him to release whatever is on his mind. He can work through it with music or paint. Fortunately, he had been blessed with positive results and was able to sell his art and music. Thankfully, after a few hours he felt relieved and started the beginnings of a song for his next CD. After pondering on a title, he decided to call it *Morning in the Desert.*

Putting away his guitar and other writing materials, he heard the clock chime one o'clock. Without realizing it, he had worked through the morning. After a quick lunch of some fruit and homemade bread from his sister, Lou, he showered and went into the studio to begin some general housekeeping. Before he starts a new project, it always helps him to clear away all the previous clutter so he can start with fresh ideas and materials.

The center worktable was littered with tubes of paint, some left open. Slick, oily paint oozed out onto the table. His expensive paint brushes, now stiff with dried paint, were left scattered where he dropped them. *What the hell is wrong with me? I never leave my studio looking like this. All this distraction is wreaking havoc with my usual routine.*

Joe began trying to salvage what he could from his paint tubes and brushes. They would need to soak several hours in cleaning solution before they could be restored to their soft, supple resiliency that he relied on for his work. He gathered several framed stretched canvases that found their way to various places around the studio and stacked them all against one wall behind a wooden screen. He would eventually add these with a few others to take to Lee for display in his gallery. While he worked, he swung open the large picture windows in the studio to let in what little breeze there was for some fresh air. All the paint fumes and cleaning solutions were making him light-headed.

He wanted to start on a couple of new sketches from ideas he thought about as he was writing music earlier. From the apparent success of his last show at Lee's, incorporating his music and art together left him with a renewed verve and gave him the impetus to get started on something new.

At times while he worked, the reoccurring memory of Rae caressing his hands continued to stalk him with the ethereal feeling of her presence. Her unknowing ability to turn something so casual into something so erotic left him breathless and surprisingly needful. He worked even more diligently for the next several hours, as he concentrated his efforts to put the studio back to working order.

⧼∰⧽

I don't remember much about driving home from Joe's house. When I pulled into my garage, I realized, fortunately, that I made it without having an accident. My thoughts had remained on him, the unusual circumstances of our meeting, his invitation to his studio, and my feelings of ease and comfort in his home. They hung over my shoulder like a warm, familiar mantle. I remember thinking that I should have been more nervous about meeting him, but I wasn't. When I sat with him and held his hands, I felt complete peace, like that was where I should be, as if we should be together. Strangely enough, when he asked me to stay, I wanted to say yes. I have never met any man who I immediately felt so connected to, or such desire for. I suddenly realized, that it was the painting that first sparked a connection with my past. At that moment, nothing else mattered to me except finding out what all of these things meant and how they came together at this point in time.

I thought back to my first marriage. Why had I even gotten married? I never even loved him. How could I? I didn't even know what love was all about, much less getting married. Robert was ten years older than me and a patient man. I think he realized the marriage wasn't going to work out long before I did. I was always searching for that shadow of a man I couldn't find. I thought I had found him in Robert, but I discovered too late that I was only trying to make everyone happy but myself. My family wanted so much for me to be happy and have a family of my own, but it was not to be. Not then. I almost lost my family once. I lost a marriage and now I was losing myself in a flood of emotion once again.

I woke from my thoughts with a start by the sound of distant coyotes and realized I was still sitting in my car. With a sudden chill coming over me, I made my way into the welcoming comfort of the house after disarming the alarm system. I moved into this house after my divorce and had the security alarm installed at the persistent pleas of my mother. My parents offered to have me move back with them, but I wanted to be on my own. I needed a quiet place and was looking forward to being independent. *God, I'm so tired!* It felt as if I had been gone for days. Things were as I left them, books and newspapers scattered on the dining room table and a cup of cold, stale tea beside my computer. When I drove to town earlier in the day, I left the wooden shutters of my windows open. Usually, the first thing I do when I come home is turn on music. Now I went from room to room and closed each shutter against the evening's darkness. Walking back to the living room, I recalled something I saw at Joe's house that looked familiar. I went to my CD stack and looked through my collection. After several minutes, I found what I was looking for. I thought I recognized a CD cover lying on his tabletop; I now looked at the same one. His *Desert Delights* was a favorite of mine and I listen to it frequently as I'm unwinding from the day. I sat back on my heels and stared at this aberration in my hands. How many times have

I listened to his music and was moved to tears of peace and joy? I have always believed that things happen in one's life for a reason, but this man has been a veiled part of my life for years and I had never met him until a few days ago. A chill returned and went up my arms, making my skin tingle.

I put the CD into the player and waited for the music to begin. I sat in the middle of the room and let it sweep over me, like a wave of relaxation. I felt a quiver start in my pelvis and radiate out toward my fingers and feet. After this sensation passed, I let out a sigh and shook myself back to the present. I let the music continue to play as I turned and remembered the painting.

The painting had not been hung yet. It sat on the floor against the wall in my office. I knew now where I needed to hang it. I picked it up like a small child and held it close to my chest. I walked down the hall to my bedroom. My heart raced like it did when I had my arms around Joe. Once, in my bedroom, I sat with it in the middle of my king-size bed and looked at each wall, trying to decide where the painting should be hung. The space directly across from me had remained void of decoration since I moved into this house several years ago.

I'm not one for wallpaper, so I left it empty, with only a chaise lounge near the window. This is one of my favorite places to read in the house. Because of the natural light of the window, I can see and hear the birds from my backyard feeders. I try to read outside when I can to enjoy my backyard, which is filled with birds and trees. I decided that my painting would occupy this space on my bedroom wall. *Yes, this will be the first thing I see every morning and the last thing I see at night.*

When I woke up the next morning, I remembered a vague dream of being at Canyon Lake. It was a warm and sunny day and I swam to the safety buoy. On the way back, a speedboat came too close and I had to dive to avoid being struck. I don't think I made it because I began to sink toward the dark, deep bottom.

I began to think I couldn't pull myself up. I saw a hand reach through the surface, grabbing my outstretched hand, and pull me upward. When my head broke the surface, I saw a familiar face. Joe Sullivan was hauling my limp body into his boat.

I awoke with a start and wasn't sure where I was. I lay there, looking at the painting, which I hung the night before, on the wall across from my bed. I threw back the jumble of covers and walked across the cool, wooden floor to stand in front of the painting. I stared at it, as if waiting for it to speak to me. Feeling as if the painting finally found its home, it helped to rid me of the fear and apprehension I felt in my bones. I now knew I had found what I was looking for.

Noticing the light filtering in from my closed shutters, I realized how late I had slept. I raced through my morning routine and had a short workout; a run on a nearby desert trail, thinking it would help clear the cobwebs from my frazzled brain. Today, I was meeting my parents to return a long lost gift.

17

The Gift

ICALLED MY PARENTS EARLIER that day to find out if they'd be home. I asked if they would mind a visit from me later in the afternoon. I wanted to show them something. Because my parents were retired, they were able to enjoy traveling and spending time with their children and grandchildren. My family spent most holidays, birthdays, anniversaries, and other special times together.

Mom said, "We'll be home all day. Please come in time for lunch."

"I'm running late, but I'll be over as soon as I can," I said as I pulled off my sweat socks and shorts I wore for my morning run. I took a quick shower and grabbed a cup of hot tea to drink on the way.

On my drive to their house, my thoughts were scattered, to say the least, trying to figure out how I was going to tell them about my discovery. I knew without a doubt it would be a shock. I remembered a few months ago, during one of our family dinners, the subject came up about swimming lessons for Terri's youngest son, Philip.

"I'll be so glad when Philip finishes his lessons. I'm a nervous wreck with him in the pool. He's doing well, but I'm not comfortable with his ability to swim safely yet."

"Why don't you let me work with him a few weeks, Terri? I'm sure he needs just a little more time and he'll do fine. You know I still have my lifeguard and CPR certificate up to date," Jack added.

"I know I shouldn't be so worried, but it seems like every day I hear on the news about another child drowning. I know, Jack, that you have devoted your life to teaching children to swim ever since our own near drowning. You are wonderful to help me. Thanks, I'll talk to Philip tomorrow."

"No problem, little sister. I'll be glad to work with him a few extra days."

As I approached my parents' neighborhood, I wondered how Philip was coming with his lessons. They were as concerned about their grandchildren's water safety as anyone. Ironically, they themselves never learned to swim and stayed well away from water. This time of year, I knew the topic would be fresh in their minds. I wondered how they would take the news I was about to deliver to them.

When I pulled up into the driveway my father, John, came out to meet me and greeted me with a hug. "How are you doing, honey? It's good to see you." My mother, Anna, not far behind, came out from the kitchen. Both my parents, now over sixty, enjoyed good health and didn't look their ages. Dad hadn't changed much over the years, except to add a few pounds here and there to his short five-foot, seven-inch frame. Slight wisps of gray feathers began to appear at his temples, despite his full head of hair. Mom maintained her slim figure by daily walking and weekly yoga classes.

"Sorry, I'm late. I overslept. I hope I didn't keep your lunch waiting." I didn't have any appetite for food just yet. My stomach was in tight knots of anticipation.

"Yes, we did, but I made you a sandwich for when you feel like eating. It's good to see you honey, I miss you when I don't hear from you for a few days." Mom's worried look reminded me to be better at my weekly phone calls. She knows my work schedule as an elementary school teacher doesn't leave much free time. I've also been trying to finish the children's picture book I've been working on.

Before I left my house, I put the shoebox in a large shopping bag to conceal it somewhat before I was ready to share it.

"How you doing?" my dad asked.

"I'm doing better. This weekend I plan to relax and catch up on my sleep and reading." That sounded so good, but I knew it wasn't going to happen due to the sudden turn of events that occurred in the last few days.

During my light lunch, they filled me in on current family events. My brother, Jack, teaches at a junior high school in town. My sister, Kate, runs her own hair salon, and my youngest sister, Terri, has three children and works at their elementary school as a teacher's aide. It became apparent that I had been out of touch with everyone. A lull in the conversation allowed me to bring out my shopping bag with its surprising contents. I had to shoo their dog, Duncan, away from it several times, as he had his nose in the bag. I'm sure he smelled something unusual.

"Dad," I said, "I came across something you might be interested in." Mom reached across the table for the remote control and turned the TV off. She wore a curious expression on her face as she moved closer to the shopping bag that she now saw sitting on the floor next to my chair.

All three of us were sitting at the small table in the family room. I pulled the shopping bag closer to where I sat and Dad leaned over with interest to get a better look.

I watched them carefully as I took out the old shoebox and sat it on the table. My Mom looked at me and then the box and then at me again. They both glanced at each other with a bewildered look on their faces and waited for me to explain.

"Do you remember a few months ago when we were talking about our Canyon Lake experience? Well, last week when I was at the Scottsdale ArtWalk, I found a painting of Canyon Lake." The shoebox remained under my hand. They both looked at each other again and then at me.

"Well, I bought the painting. The more I thought about it, the more convinced I became that I had to have it. I went back to the gallery last week and bought it." A look of surprise came over my parents' faces. I had not ever made such an extravagant purchase before.

"That's great, Rae! Where are you going to hang it? We'd love to see it."

"I hung it on the wall in my bedroom. It was the

only place that had enough wall space, and I wanted to be able to look at it every day."

My hand rested on the lid of the shoebox and my fingertips could feel the indentations of age and the thin layer of dust that accumulated over the years from being stored in Joe's closet. I moved my fingers to the edge and lifted the lid as I continued to talk. I watched their faces to see when their eyes would be drawn to its contents. I wanted to see what kind of expression or reaction they might have. When I lifted the lid fully off, the faint aroma of stale green moss and lake water wafted toward me and into the room. The memory of this smell from the night before came back to me, as I looked at their faces to see if they were able to pick up the same scent.

My dad sat closest to the shoebox. He leaned forward and I could tell that he smelled something unusual. His face had a pinched expression and he rubbed his hand across his face. He looked up at me and said, "What are those?"

"Do they look familiar?" I asked.

"They look like the kind I used to wear, they look like . . ." his voice stopped and he looked from me to Mom and back to me. My mom had peered into the shoebox by this time, let out a gasp, and covered her mouth with her hand, tears welling in her eyes.

As the realization formed in their minds, tears came to my eyes, and all three of us were drawn back to 1967 in the old Comet station wagon. Our hands found each other around the table and held tight, tears welling in our eyes. When we finally sat back and took a breath, my dad asked, "How can this be, where did they come from? I thought I lost these years ago."

After I regained my voice, I said, "Yes, I know. I thought they were lost forever, too. Something amazing happened." I paused to take a drink of water and clear the lump in my throat. I continued, "The man who saved you that day took these from the lake to return them to you, but we had already started to leave. He asked me to give them to you now."

They both sat with shocked looks on their faces. My dad made a struggled motion to speak, but no words came out. My mother uttered a muffled whimper and reached for my hand again.

"What?" my dad said incredulously as his voice returned. "You mean you spoke to the man who pulled us out? Come on, is this some kind of a joke, Rae? Do you know how many times I have wondered about this person?"

I nodded my head. "Yes, we have all wanted to know more about him. I met him. I know it's hard to believe, but he's the one who painted *Canyon Lake,* the painting that I now own."

They both started talking at once and, after they were convinced that it could be true, I spent the next several hours retelling the events of the past week. I felt drained, but I also had a feeling of elation as I shared with my parents how I came to meet this shadow of a man who had been a vital part of our family, but who we never knew.

As the afternoon wore on, they of course wanted to meet him and I told them I would convey their request, but not to expect it. "He is a very busy man," I told them.

Why did I say that? He wanted to meet me. I know I was stalling for time. Maybe they would be satisfied knowing about him and let it go. Who was I kidding!

As I drove home that evening, I was more tired than I expected, and found myself looking forward to a quiet evening on my patio watching the desert end its day. But that was not to be. I found a message on my answering machine from Joe asking me to call him. He left his phone number for me in case I misplaced it from last night. Not only had I not misplaced it, it was burned into my memory, just like my childhood memory of that day on the lake.

Before I called him I had to make a choice. Do I keep this new adventure just an adventure, or does it have potential to develop into a relationship?

Yes, I needed a little adventure. Lord knows it had been awhile since I treated myself to meeting new people. And yes, I was ready for a new friendship or relationship. I hadn't seen anyone seriously since my divorce last year.

I have been a little cautious in that department because I wasn't ready to delve into any kind of a tailspin arrangement again! My divorce, after a short marriage of eighteen months, left me feeling a little vulnerable and wary about getting involved again too quickly. At this stage of my life, I did not want to put myself at risk again for a breakup. The irony of it all made me laugh to myself. Now it seemed that I had two men interested in me at the same time, although Lee's interest seemed a bit too threatening and made me feel uneasy. Sometime soon I would have to ask Joe what he knew about him.

Maybe I was thinking too far ahead. I just needed to step back and take it slow. The least I could do is call Joe back and find out what he wanted. Lee, on the other hand, will require a little more thought.

18

~⎯MMM⎯⌒

The Drive

J OE WAITED AS LONG as he could. His wall clock told him it was after five. He needed to talk to her. He walked from room to room, picking things up and straightening the place as he went. He couldn't concentrate on his sketches anymore. He worked several hours on a sketch that later turned out to be of Rae standing at the wide expanse of windows, looking out at the desert. Standing back to take a better look, he realized how closely he captured her look of radiant beauty as it reflected back from the desert behind her. Thin, wavy blonde strands of her hair began to fall free of the wooden pick she held it up with, and the smile on her lips showed a trace of a hidden secret that only she knew about. *God, I remember those dark blue eyes that seemed to go to my core and make me shudder, as if someone put an icy finger on the pulse of my neck,* Joe thought.

When he dialed her number, it rang several times before the answering machine clicked on. Her voice was as he remembered it. It did not have the casual, relaxed tone from last evening. He quickly left a message asking her to call him when she got in. He breathed a sigh of relief when he realized he would have some additional time to think about what he would say next. Just being around her stirred something in him that he had not felt in a long time. With a tightness in his chest and a stirring in his groin, he paced the room. *Oh God, where was I headed? Was I ready for her to be a part of my life? Yes, Joe. Wake up. Whether you like it or not, she already is a part of your life.*

Joe heard the phone ring later that evening while sitting on the back patio, enjoying the sweet smelling desert air. He had taken the portable phone with him and sat it on the patio table so that he would be sure to hear it. He brought his guitar out and sat strumming it, just to keep his hands busy. He felt unusually nervous and was able to relax a bit by letting his mind wander through the music. As he reached for the phone, he paused and stared at it, knowing it was Rae. He had to somehow convince her to see him again without thinking he was some kind of nut. Then it all became clear.

"Hello," he said as clearly as possible, considering the present state of his mind and body.

"Hi Joe, this is Rae. I hope I'm not calling too late."

"No, not at all, I'm glad you called," he said, trying to clear the dryness from his throat. "Thanks for calling back. Did you have a good day?"

"Yes, as a matter of fact, it was an interesting day. I told my parents about you and gave them the shoes. I'll tell you about it someday."

"Oh yes, the moccasins. I would like to hear about it." Joe paused, taking a breath, before continuing. "I don't know what you usually have planned for Sundays, but if you're free, would you like to take a drive with me?"

"Okay, that sounds nice. I like Sunday drives. Where to?"

"Oh, I have a place in mind. It's somewhere you're familiar with."

"You're not going to tell me? You're going to make me guess?"

"I'm sure you'll figure it out soon enough. I'll pick you up around ten. We can grab something to drink while we drive first, if you like."

"That sounds great. Do you need my address and directions?"

"An address would be helpful. I have a good city map and should be able to find it."

"Okay. Ready? It's 20811 S. Greenfield. Call me if you get lost."

"Great! I'll see you tomorrow"

"Bye Joe, and thanks."

"Thanks for what?"

"Just thanks."

When he hung up, Joe sat back in the chair and stared out his back patio, looking into the desert. He said to himself as he took a deep breath, *Well, Joe, now you have to see this thing through. God, help me.*

⚬─✠✠✠⚬

That night, as I lay listening to the desert's evening noises of crickets and the occasional yip of a distant coyote, sleep finally came to me around midnight. My short conversation with Joe did not make me rest any easier. *What was this "drive" all about? Maybe it would give*

us some time away from the painting, and we could find out
more about each other after all these years.

With the morning light peeking through the cracks
of my wooden shuttered windows, I woke with a start
from that distressing water dream again. *Damn, when is*
this going to stop? Maybe after Joe and I finish talking and
find out what we need to know, I'll be able to finally put this
behind me.

I came out of the shower and was towel drying my
hair when the doorbell rang. I thought I would have
more time because I was sure it would take him at least
an hour to find my place without directions. It was almost twenty miles southwest of his place.

I yelled though the door, "Coming," as I yanked the
towel from my hair and ran my fingers through it, trying to smooth out some of the tangles, while at the same
time trying to secure my loose robe around me.

When I opened the door, I found Joe standing there
with three soft, pink roses cradled in his hands. After I
noticed the roses, I looked into his face and found such
a look of happiness and pure joy it made me giggle like
a girl on her first date. I guess maybe I was. Until that
moment, I never really thought about it, but this was
the first time I have ever received flowers from a man.
I bought my own wedding flowers. (That probably
should have been my first clue that the marriage was
doomed.)

I reached to touch him, as a way to draw him into
the house, and he pressed the roses into my arms.
"Wow, what a surprise," I said through my continued
giggle. I'm sure my face appeared slightly flushed, as I

felt embarrassed by my sudden loss of coherent speech. "Please, come in."

"I hope you like roses," he said.

"Yes, I do. They're my favorite flower. Oh, they're beautiful. Pink roses symbolize admiration, I believe. Is that why you chose them?" I bent my head and dipped my nose closer to smell their sweet aroma.

"In a way, I guess I did. I thought of you when I saw them. I did get three for a reason though; one is for our past, one is for our present, and one is for our future. I hope you don't mind."

I noticed a slow, red flush creep up from his neck to his chin. "No, I don't mind. That's a lovely thought." I tried to hide the warm feeling that came over me by changing the subject. I turned my face away, suddenly realizing it revealed too much of what I was feeling. I could feel my body instantly respond to his nearness with a warm flush.

"Did you have any trouble finding my place?" I said, trying to regain some composure.

"Actually, no, I've been here before," he said.

I must have registered a look of surprise on my face for the second time, because he continued quickly, "No, not at the house, but at the San Tan's. I drove through the area last year and did some sketches. I finished several paintings and they're in my studio, ready to send to Lee at the gallery."

"Oh, that's great. I'm glad you found it interesting enough to want to paint. I'd like to see them sometime."

By this time, I had begun moving toward the kitchen and he followed me into my living room. His gaze left mine and he turned to stand in front of the wall-sized window facing the San Tan Mountains.

"It's no wonder you were drawn to my window, we have the same tastes in landscapes," Joe commented as we both found ourselves standing side-by-side, in a familiar pose, looking out the window.

With the sudden awareness of his closeness, I moved a step back. "Will you excuse me while I finish getting ready? You surprised me. I thought it would take you a lot longer to get here. I'll put these in some water," I said holding up the roses.

He turned toward me and studied my face. I was afraid of what he might find there. I did not yet want him to know what I was thinking or feeling. I now realized, with sudden clarity, that I wanted more than friendship from this man. I was afraid to let myself hope that here was the person who could fill the empty spot of loneliness I had been ignoring for so long.

"I didn't realize how long your hair was. The other times I've seen you, it was wrapped up." He reached out to touch it and laid his hand at the back of my head, slowly letting it trail down my back. Even though I had long since dried off from my shower, my hair remained damp. I could not help but close my eyes and give into the shivering sensation that came over me. As his hand reached the end of my hair and rested at the base of my spine, I came out of my reverie and remembered that he had spoken to me.

"Oh . . . yes. I usually wear it in a coil when I am working; it's easier and stays out of my way."

"Would you leave it down today, for me?" His eyes moved from mine and roamed my face. I stood there, watching him follow the contours of my face. His steel-blue eyes found mine and all I could do was shake my head yes.

I moved away slowly from the window and made my way to the bedroom to finish getting ready, trying not to trip over my own rubbery feet. I stopped in the kitchen to get a vase for the roses and brought them with me into the bedroom. I sat them on the small reading stand near the window so I could glance at them frequently. I tried to shake myself back into reality, but had a difficult time re-membering what I was supposed to be doing. He had left me shaken. *Come on, Rae. Get a hold of yourself.*

⟿〰〰

When Rae left the room, Joe remained a few more mo-ments at the window and contemplated the day ahead. *I hope she wasn't offended by the roses. She looked a little startled by them. In fact, I think she liked them. Maybe it's been awhile since anyone gave her flowers. Anyway, I like roses. They remind me of Rae, soft and sensitive to the touch, yet she is still wary of me for some reason. I hope after today her feelings will change.*

Without realizing how much time had passed, Rae re-turned to the window to stand beside Joe. She was wearing a suede jacket, soft with age, that had a silver and turquoise dragonfly pin attached to the lapel. Her jeans fit snugly in all the right places and well-used walking boots, scuffed from long use, completed her comfortable demeanor. She stood close enough that their arms brushed against each other. Joe could smell the subtle perfume she wore as well as her fresh washed hair, which now hung loose. As he turned toward her, he looked into her face to find dazzling blue eyes and a slight upturned curve to her mouth. His breath caught in his throat as he took in her serene and tranquil beauty. He had to fight a sudden impulse to touch her, wanting to capture some of that unseen spirit that seemed to be emitting from her like pheromones. *What is it about her that draws me to her like a moth to a flame?*

"You are so beautiful Rae. You and your surroundings seem to fit together well."

"Oh, thank you . . ." her voice trailed off as Joe stepped away from her.

He stepped back in order to keep himself from wrapping her in his arms and never letting go.

He now completed his first glimpse at the large room that was obviously well-used. She watched as he made a visual 360-degree turn around the room. Even though it was full of books and stacked with other miscellaneous works in progress, it appeared to be organized in some fashion that only she could comprehend.

"Oh, don't mind my confused-looking work space, it's actually quite organized," she commented.

"No doubt," Joe replied. "Do you bring all of your work home with you?"

"I try to do most of my school work on campus. I am also a self-proclaimed bibliophile, adding to my ever-increasing book collection. And on top of everything else, I'm trying to write a children's book."

"It looks as if creative minds like ours don't always keep a tidy house. Well, if you're ready, let's go."

"Yes, I'm ready. Where are we headed?"

"I told you it's a surprise, remember?"

Joe waited for me at the front steps while I locked the door and set the alarm. We turned toward the Jeep and our hands found each other naturally. Our fingers entwined together as we walked down the sidewalk to his nearby Jeep. I looked up at him and saw a slightly upturned smile as he looked down at me and gave my hand a slight, reassuring squeeze.

He held the door open for me and I settled into his Jeep. I began to relax and enjoy the last of the cool summer morning, the time just before the hot air takes over the day. As Joe started up the Jeep for our day's journey, I doubted that I would need my jacket. Looking back through the side mirror, I could see dust being churned up from the gravel driveway when we left my house.

We headed back toward town in a northeasterly direction. I still hadn't a clue as to our destination; at this point, I didn't care. I was enjoying the spontaneity of the day. My thoughts were pulled back quickly to the present by Joe brushing against the side of my leg, trying to get my attention.

"Where are you, Rae? I asked you three questions and you haven't heard one of them."

"Oh Joe, I'm sorry. I was just daydreaming and thinking about what a glorious morning this is. What did you ask me?"

"That's all right. I wanted you to tell me about your children's book. What's it about and when will it be finished?"

"Well, this is my first attempt, so it's going pretty slow. It's about two children who are lost in the mountains and a wolf pack who leads them to safety. I hope to have it finished by next summer."

"Sounds like a good adventure."

"I hope so. How are you coming on your paintings and music?"

A slow grin appeared on Joe's face and he began to chuckle.

"Well, it's funny you should ask. Lee called and asked me the same question. He wants more artwork for the gallery and he's received a call from a local massage therapist who wants to use my music during her sessions. Now I just need to find the time to get it all done."

Now that the subject came up, here was my chance to ask Joe about Lee.

"Can I ask you a question about Lee?" I turned toward Joe in the seat.

"Of course. I don't know if I'll be able to answer it or not, but go ahead." Joe continued to watch the road ahead as he answered.

"Well, I was wondering how well you know him. Do you and he do things together? Socially, I mean?"

"We've only worked together through his gallery. We haven't socialized. It never came up. We have both been busy trying to make a go of our businesses. Why do you ask?" Now Joe turned his head to look at me in the face.

⁓᷍᷍᷍⁓

Without realizing it, her brows came together with a pained look that showed visible distress.

"Rae, what is it? Has something happened?"

"Maybe it's nothing, but he called me and asked me out to lunch. I had an uneasy feeling about it."

"Did you go?" Joe realized for the first time that he really didn't know Lee all that well personally and, since they didn't do things together socially, he had no idea how he was around women.

"No. I told him that I couldn't. I'd already made plans

for that day. I suggested we meet some other time, but now I'm not so sure. That's why I wanted to ask you about him."

"Rae, if you have any concerns about him at all, don't feel like you have to apologize. Besides, I want to be the one to take you to lunch. Okay?" Joe was hoping to see more of Rae. He had no idea Lee had been talking to her.

Joe watched the road as Rae continued to stare out the window. He wondered what she was really thinking about. Their conversation about Lee had temporarily taken her mind off where they were going. Surprisingly, she hadn't recognized where they were headed. Joe was anxious to see what kind of reaction she would have once she recognized their destination. There wasn't much traffic yet, so he easily made good time. It was his hope to get there before Rae told him to turn around. Joe had no way of knowing how long it had been since she last visited the lake, but felt it was time for both of them to go back.

As Joe made his way up the mountain, Rae turned to look at him. There was no mistaking the uneasy and worried look that came across her face.

"Joe, where are we going?"

"Do you recognize the place?"

"Yes, of course I do, but why are you taking me here?"

As she looked at him, he could tell she was trying to decide whether to make him turn around or keep going. By the time she opened her mouth to protest, he was pulling into the parking lot. When he turned off the engine, all became quiet. His Jeep was not the only vehicle in the lot on this Sunday morning. Joe sat looking at her and reached for her hand.

"Rae, it's time we both faced that awful day. We can do this together. Will you help me?"

Rae slumped back in the seat and slowly nodded her head.

19

The Return

WHEN I REALIZED WHERE we were going, it was too late to ask Joe to turn around. In a way, I'm glad he kept going. I have wanted many times to make the trip up there, but always found a reason not to. Now, at least he was with me to help steady my nerves.

When we pulled into the parking lot, he came around my side of the Jeep to help me out. His hand was warm as it took hold of mine. I felt a great relief knowing that on this trip there would be no young children screaming in terror for their parents as there had been in my past.

The first thing I noticed as we started walking toward the water's edge was the beauty and immensity of the canyon walls. Huge waves of rock towered over me as I looked from one end of the canyon to the other. My memory erased the forgotten beauty of the canyon. My mind went back to Joe's painting and I smiled to myself, knowing that he had captured it so accurately.

Even now, more than thirty years later, the surrounding area of the canyon hadn't changed much. My perception of the area as a child was very different than now, as I returned to it as an adult. I am sure as a child it became a delightful, watery playland. In reality, it is a dirt-beach, rocky scrub-brush desert. The cliff wall is, however, spectacular with a multitude of colors streaking across its rocks.

"The canyon is so colorful. With all the rain we had this year, it made the trees green and all the desert plants bloom bright." A faint desert smell of creosote and mossy effervescence floated past me on the breeze.

"It's no wonder you wanted to paint this place," I said as I scanned the panoramic view.

"Actually, when I first did the sketches for it, it wasn't this green. I came back later in the spring to look at it again before I filled in all the color."

While we continued to make our way to the shoreline, I soon noticed that the State Parks Department had done its best to make some improvements to the area over the years. The parking lot and covered ramadas, complete with concrete picnic tables, were a welcome addition since I was here last, but, unfortunately, the so-called beach remained in a sad state. It consisted mostly of rocky ground and very little sand.

I paused for a moment and looked out over the lake. The only water buoys I saw were those strung in a line, indicating the traffic lane for boats and other watercraft. We stopped walking and stood side-by-side, looking out over the water. I spotted a few dragonflies playing tag with other insects on the surface of the water. Joe held my hand; maybe he felt I would run. He gave my hand a squeeze and I looked at him.

"I think this is the place," Joe told me.

"How can you be so sure? I'm not sure I even re-member."

"See the way the beach bends into this cove? I was on my inner tube just up a ways." He pointed toward the west. "I came floating down this direction when I heard your screams." I followed the direction of his hand as he pointed.

We were now standing at the water's edge and I could look down and see maybe two feet out and then black water. I took another step forward and Joe grabbed my arm, holding me back.

"I think you're right." When I leaned forward I could see what looked like the edge of a cliff.

"I can see how your father stepped right off the edge. If you're not looking for it, you go right in." Joe stepped closer and peered over, trying to get a better look at the seemingly bottomless pit not two feet from where we stood. I automatically reached out and grabbed the black leather belt he wore within the loops of his jeans. Even though we were both good swimmers, I did not want a reoccurring episode of my childhood nightmare.

"Why aren't there any warning buoys around here?" I asked rhetorically. I was aghast that even now there were no signs warning of the hazard.

We both stepped away from the edge and walked to the nearest shaded picnic table and sat down. We sat close together, absorbed in our own thoughts. Joe put his arm protectively around my shoulders and pulled me closer. I leaned into him and rested my head on his shoulder, waiting for the thud in my chest to go away. I don't know what I expected, but I never would have be-lieved I would be sitting here with the man who saved my family's life. The afternoon bloomed a calm, blue sky that contrasted the feelings that ran through me. I felt anger at myself for not being able to do more to help my parents. The four of us young kids were totally helpless. I remember knowing and feeling the immense danger I would be putting myself in if I tried to help them, so I stayed with my siblings. Joe must have experienced his own living hell to witness what he did with his own family and not be able to do anything.

Joe seemed to sense my feelings because he said, "You know, you couldn't have done anything. If I hadn't been the first one there, you know someone else would have come to help."

"Yes, I know that now, but how much time would they have had?" I said to him with tears in my eyes.

"I don't know, but I'm glad I was there and able to help," he said as I got up and started walking toward the shore again.

⟜╼⟝

I stood for several moments with my arms wrapped around my chest, as if trying to protect myself from the cold, even though it was a warm day. When Joe came to stand beside me at the water's edge, I asked, "How are you feeling about all this? I know that you can never turn back time, but does it help you at all knowing that you helped my family when you couldn't have helped your stepfather?"

Joe stood behind me with his arms around me, as he looked over my head and out toward the water. He took a deep breath and turned me around so that I was now looking into his face.

"Yes, Rae. I think that it has helped me a lot. First, finding you, and then, being able to put all my guilt behind me."

I turned to face the water again with him pressed to my back and his arms circled protectively around me.

"Thanks for bringing me here. I needed to see this place again. I feel like I have some closure on this episode in my life and now I'm ready to get on with the rest of it," I said.

He moved and stood beside me.

⁓〰⁓

She looked up at him with sparkling blue eyes full of expectation and asked, "Will you be a part of it now?"

Joe turned toward her and cupped her face in his hands and gently kissed her lips, then her neck, and then her ears, smelling the essence of her skin and hair as he made his way to the nape of her neck. She tilted her head into his shoulder and he felt her shiver as she tightened her arms around him.

"Yes," he said with a sigh of relief. He pulled away from her and held her face between his hands. "It's like finding my way home after a long journey."

20

The Way Back

JOE'S KISS WAS MORE than I expected in the way of an answer, but one that confirmed my feelings. I knew now, without a doubt, that he meant a great deal to me, and I would do all I could to keep him from walking out of my life again.

The drive home was one of shared conversation about our work, passions, and futures. I asked him about his work and how he got started. I was interested because I wanted to find out how much this particular experience affected his work, if any.

"After my mother died, my sister Lou moved out here to be close to me. This was after her divorce and she wanted her kids to grow up with what little family she had left. She, of course, never blamed me for what happened to her father. Lou always knew that he died of a heart attack at the lake where we grew up, but was really too young to understand the guilt I carried around by not being able to do something. My mother was at a loss as to how to help me because she was dealing with her own guilt and grief. It was something I had to work through myself. That's why I decided to go to college out of state and ended up moving to Arizona. Teaching helped to keep me occupied for several years, but as I grew older, it was my painting and music that really aided me in learning how to release the guilt that built up over the years. I thought I had finally put it all behind me and was starting to take my life back when you suddenly appeared. Rae, you made me realize that all of these events happened to us for a reason. That we were supposed to come together and help one another heal those old wounds." I sat quietly and let him talk until he stopped and took his eyes off the road long enough to glance at me. From the pained expression on his face, he looked as if he hadn't slept in a week.

⌐⟋⟍⟍⟍⟍⟍⟍⟍⟍⟍⟍⟍⟍⟍⟍⟍⟍⟍⟍

My family had always been an important part of what I do. Maybe it was because I was given a second chance and I didn't want to waste it. Once in town, we decided to stop for lunch in Scottsdale at an out-of-the-way cafe to continue our quiet conversation and then headed for the downtown shops. Joe wanted to show me some of the other paintings he had at Lee's place and then walk through some of the other galleries around Scottsdale. We both needed to get out and walk for a while to get our minds off of our trip to the lake.

When we pulled up in front of Lee's gallery, Joe looked over at me and winked. "Are you ready? Are you comfortable going in?" he asked, remembering my earlier question about Lee.

I said, "Yes, as long as you're with me. Are you okay with Lee? I mean, I hope this won't disrupt your business with him."

He reassured me of his answer by leaning over and kissing me full on the mouth. When our faces came together, I could smell remnants from Canyon Lake. I breathed in deeply to absorb as much of his scent as possible. I could do nothing but give into it and kiss him back, secretly hoping there would be more of these warm, lingering kisses. When Joe broke away, I still had my eyes closed, wanting to keep his taste and touch with me. When I sensed him move, I opened my eyes and watched him get out of the Jeep. I sat back in the seat and did not move until he opened my door.

"Come on. Lee likes surprises," he said as he came around my side of the Jeep to open the door. Somehow I doubted that Lee liked surprises, but after our morning trek to the lake, I was ready to face anything with Joe.

As we entered the gallery holding hands, Lee looked up from his paperwork with a somewhat astonished expression on his face. I'm sure he was used to seeing Joe come in unannounced, but I could tell by the look on his face that he seldom, if ever, saw him come in with a woman holding his hand. Joe released me long enough to greet Lee with a handshake as he rose from his desk.

"Well, Joe, this is a surprise. I didn't expect to see you today," Lee said, making his way around his desk to stand in front of us.

"I'm sure it is. I hope you don't mind that we just dropped in. Lee, you remember Rae Warner. She's the woman who bought *Canyon Lake* last week."

"Yes, I remember, nice to see you again Rae."

"Thank you, Lee. It's nice to see you again."

"Well, it looks like you two have been spending a lot of time together lately. Joe, I've been trying to get a hold of you. I've got some potential clients who are very interested in your work. They want to meet with you."

"Yes, Lee, you're right. I have been spending a lot of time with Rae and hope to spend a lot more," Joe said as he looked over at me and gave my hand a squeeze. "I promise next week to get with you and any clients you want. Go ahead and set up an appointment. I've got several new pieces they may be interested in. Call me when you get things set up."

While Joe and Lee continued to talk about their future showings, I wandered around, looking at several pieces hung with special lighting and tasteful accents. Overstuffed chairs were carefully placed in comfortable groups that invited gallery-goers to sit and enjoy their surroundings while deciding on their purchase. Most of the paintings and sculptures depicted a Southwest aura in their presentation that appealed to my sense of aesthetics. While I meandered around, I found myself in the back, out of public view. I noticed an "Employees Only" sign attached to a wide, solid-colored black door. What caught my eye was that it was different from all the other doors in the gallery. The other doors were hand-carved, wooden Southwest doors with intricate handles. This door appeared to be solid metal with a sturdy silver handle. When I walked closer and touched it, I discovered that it was in fact metal and slightly opened. A cool blast of air coming from below diverted my eyes momentarily from a flashing green light on the alarm panel next to it. I stood for a moment, leaning forward to look through the small crack in the opening. Lee came to stand behind me. His large, muscular forearm brushed past my face and pushed the door closed.

Before it swung shut, I caught a glimpse of the stairs leading down. When I turned to face him, a sudden, brilliant flash of light blinded me.

"Sorry to startle you, Rae. I thought this would be a good time for me to take your picture. I always like to take a photograph of all my clients. You know . . . for my scrapbook." His sardonic chuckle didn't convince me of his good intentions.

"This is just my security vault where I keep artists' work until it's ready to display. You don't want to go down there," Lee said, as if to answer the question on my face. He then grabbed my arm, in a not too gentle manner, and ushered me toward the front of the gallery.

"I'm sorry, Lee. I guess I got sidetracked when I was looking at things and didn't realize where I was. Please forgive me," I said, hoping that this would reassure him and he would release my arm.

I heard the door chime in the background and hoped that Joe hadn't decided to wait for me outside. A cold chill fluttered in my stomach.

"Come on," he said, "you don't want to keep Joe waiting." Lee led me around the corner into the front area of the gallery and I saw Joe waiting for me at the front door.

"Are you ready to go?" Joe asked.

By the time I had stepped into Joe's view, Lee had released my arm. I said, "Yes," and we headed toward the entrance. Lee was talking to some people who had just entered the gallery. Joe and Lee must have already said their goodbyes because this time Joe put his arm around me and we walked through the front door.

When we stepped out into the bright afternoon sun, Joe asked me, "Are you all right? Did Lee say something?"

"No, he didn't say anything, and yes, I'm fine." I wasn't ready to tell Joe about my unexpected "photo session" with Lee just yet. "I just wandered into the back room and it was obvious that he didn't want me there. Did you know he has a vault back there?" I looked at Joe to see what kind of a response I would get.

"Yeah, I knew he had a vault. Most of the galleries around here have one somewhere. They use it to store the more valuable pieces that come from various artists. For insurance purposes, they are usually required to have some kind of vault or security system."

"Okay," I said to Joe, shaking off the last remnant feeling of Lee's hand on my arm. I covered the spot on my arm where he grabbed me and felt sure I would have a bruise there in the morning.

I reached for Joe's hand and said, "Take me on that tour you promised." I knew this would be no ordinary tourist gallery walk. By the time our afternoon came to a close, I discovered I was not disappointed. Joe had taken me into several shops that were not on any gallery tour map. These were exhibits that not only showed the "latest and greatest" up-and-coming names, but "invitation only" showings as well. Joe was greeted warmly wherever we went. He evidently had not told me everything about his popularity in the local art scene. A whole new world opened up before me and I felt like a wilted flower, refreshed after drinking it all in.

I was thoroughly exhausted and yet exhilarated by all that I had seen by the time we walked back to the

Jeep. The sun began to set and the sky was full of vivid softness.

"Are you ready to go to dinner?" Joe asked as he started the Jeep.

"Yes, I'm famished. But, if you don't mind, let's go back to my place. I can fix us something to eat there. Would that be all right with you?"

"That sounds great to me, if you're sure," he said.

"Yes, I'm sure," I said. After a tentative moment, I reached over and kissed his soft, full lips. His touch was as needful as mine, as he pulled me into him. Our lips responded automatically to each other, parting, allowing our tongues to taste and explore one another with anticipation.

It was several minutes before Joe started the Jeep and we headed east toward my house, wondering what would become of the night ahead.

21

The Apple

THE HOUSE INSIDE WAS dark by the time we arrived. I didn't leave on any interior lights because I thought I would be back before dark. The security lights had come on at the front and rear of the house and lit our way down the driveway. Joe parked the Jeep in front and got out to open my door. We paused for a moment before we went in and stood arm in arm listening to the quietness that fell around us. I closed my eyes and tilted my head upward to breathe in the cool air that began to form as the desert embarked on its evening repose.

After entering the house and disarming the alarm, I quickly lit some candles and turned on a few lights, giving the house a warm glow. I went to the wall unit that housed my CD player and started Joe's disc that I had been listening to earlier. When the music started, he came and stood behind me, encircling me with his arms. He leaned forward, putting his head into my hair, and nuzzled the back of my neck. This was becoming a familiar pose that I liked very much.

"I had a great day, Rae. I like spending time with you."

Still with his arms around me and his soft guitar music playing in the background, I turned toward him and we embraced in a long, slow kiss that revealed just how much we enjoyed being with each other. The flicker of passion that had started earlier began to reveal itself as we began to release our feelings for each other and gave into the long awaited sensations of pent up lust.

When we broke our embrace, I said, "I feel the same way. I feel like it's a dream and I'll wake up and you'll be gone and none of this will have happened."

"It's no dream, Rae. I'm here for you. I'll stay until you tell me to leave."

I choked back a sob and continued to press my face into his chest, fearing he would in fact vanish before my eyes.

"Oh God, Joe, I don't ever want you to leave me again," I said into his shoulder while I wrapped my arms around him, not quite ready to release him. When I stepped back and looked into his face, I was given one of his wonderful smiles, which revealed perfect teeth and the beginnings of creases at the corners of his eyes that told me everything was going to be all right.

"Okay," I said, trying to regain my composure. "Let's see how good you are in the kitchen. Can you help me with dinner?"

"Hey, I'm pretty good in the kitchen. I make one hell of a salad, so long as you've got the makings."

"Oh, I've got just what you need. Follow me," I said, hoping the pun would be overlooked. The broad smile on his face told me that he caught both of my meanings.

We ate our late supper sitting close together on the

sofa, drinking wine, as we talked into the night about our families and the friends that we made over the years. We both craved to know as much about each other as possible. Without realizing how much time had passed, a bright full moon made its ascent high over the arid landscape outside.

I got up from the sofa and stretched. "Would you like some coffee? We can sit out on the porch and enjoy the cool night."

"Thanks, but I don't need any coffee right now." The softness in Joe's voice made me turn around. He touched my shoulder and pulled me gently toward him. "Oh, Rae, don't ask me to leave tonight. Let me stay with you," he said as his mouth found mine.

When I was able to speak again, I said, "I don't want you to leave, Joe. I need you." I closed my eyes and rested my face against his chest. My body said yes to his as he picked me up and carried me to my room. I asked myself, *Do I dare take this risk of finding that I need him more than he needs me? Please, Rae, give yourself one more chance. Yes. I'll take the risk.*

When my feet found the floor again, I walked over and opened the windows slightly to let in the fresh night air and left the wooden slates of the shutters opened to let the moonlight filter into the room. I started to unbutton my shirt, but was interrupted by Joe's hands taking my place. "Let me do it, Rae. I want to undress you," Joe said as he bent his head to lightly kiss my cheek.

We helped each other undress in the moonlight, watching each other's skin appear as each piece of clothing was removed. The moonlight shining through the shuttered windows left us with pale, white streaks across our bodies, further adding to our heightened ardor. We continued to kiss and explore each other's body by touching and running our hands over each other, as if to reassure ourselves that we were real.

"Rae, your skin is glowing and so white in this moonlight. It's as if you are lit from the inside."

We lay together on the cool sheets, his body resting gently on top of mine. I moved my hands across his shoulders and down his back. I could feel him shiver and press his hips into me. He took my hands in his and stretched them over my head. When his body entered mine, sliding effortlessly, sheer fiery sensuality consumed us and we moved together, becoming one soul.

He filled me with such emotion and tenderness I could not breathe. I rested my face against his and breathed in his breath to replace mine and felt his essence fill me. Maybe because in the past our souls touched or came together in some other ethereal meeting, I could not tell, but I knew I had had found my soul mate and that, no matter what, Joe Sullivan entered my life again for the last time.

Our first night together rekindled feelings in me that I imagined were gone forever. I felt electrically charged with energy that was better than any jolt of caffeine. The passions and urgency we shared during our lovemaking were startling. We were like two souls starved for the human touch.

I woke to the early morning sun coming in through my east bedroom window. I turned over and discovered Joe on one elbow, looking over me and then at my bedside stand. I turned toward him, pushing the tangled mass of hair from my face, and raised up.

"What's the apple for?" he said as he motioned with his head.

I reached over and grabbed the apple and took a bite, then handed it to him.

"Here, take a bite," I said. He munched on the apple as I told him about an old french story of two lovers who would leave an apple on their night stand so that in the morning they could each take a bite to freshen their mouths after a night of sleep and lovemaking.

"Now, kiss me," I said after he devoured the apple.

We shared a sweet morning kiss that smelled and tasted of sweet, juicy apples. We were in no hurry to get out of bed. His mouth met mine and our kisses revived the memories of the night before. Our tongues licked the remaining juices left by the apple from our mouths. I pressed myself against him and swung my leg over him while turning him on his back. I now sat on top, straddling him, looking down at him through my tangled mass of hair. He reached up to clear the strands from my face and I caught the side of his hand with my mouth, giving him a gentle love bite. A renewed sense of urgency filled both of us, as we did not stop until we were slick with sweat and tangled in the bed sheets. I felt like I had been hanging upside-down and had the wind knocked out of me. It was as if we were both afraid of not ever being able to share this moment again.

Laying side-by-side, winded and slowly reclaiming our breath, I watched as Joe got out of bed and walked naked to my bedroom window to look out at the desert morning. Even approaching fifty, he still possessed the physique of a much younger man. His broad shoulders, narrow waist, and chest with enough hair for me to rub my face in, made my heart skip a beat.

While Joe showered, I put together some breakfast. We ate on the patio, speaking few words, but shared knowing glances with each other as we watched the desert morning come alive. Joe read the morning paper while I slipped away for a quick shower.

I was beginning to discover that everything felt so smooth and rhythmic when Joe was around me, like all of the tectonic plates have shifted and come together. Over the next few weeks, we were rarely apart. Joe made trips to and from his studio, or I went with him. He met with Lee and together they had made arrangements for another gallery showing. The subject of my having lunch with Lee never came up again and I'd forgotten to ask Joe about his "scrapbook."

Late one afternoon, while we were relaxing at his studio on the back patio, I casually said, "You know there is someone else who would like to meet you."

He looked up at me from his guitar with a slight smile on his face. "Yeah, I know. I was wondering when you were going to suggest it."

"I haven't talked to my parents since I took them the moccasins. At the time, they were very curious about you. I know they would like to meet you."

He put down his guitar and came to squat down in front of me as I sat in the lounge chair. He pulled my hands into his and said, "I'll be ready any time you are." I pulled him into my arms and we sat together watching the sunset over the mountains.

I made the phone call the next afternoon. When I

explained my weeklong absence of catching up on my writing and working extra hours at school, my parents were more than happy to see my visitor and me.

"We can stop by tomorrow afternoon, if that's okay with you?"

"Of course it is, Rae. Your father and I are looking forward to meeting Mr. Sullivan."

"Thanks, Mom. I think he's anxious to meet you as well." I hung up and called Joe with our plans for him to meet my parents. He would now be able to see for himself how important he has become to our family, and what he did for us all those years ago.

22

The Roses

JOE ARRIVED AT MY door by eleven o 'clock, looking rested from his long week of planning and preparing for the following week's show at Lee's gallery. I heard the Jeep pull up to the house and watched him navigate into the small turn-around gravel driveway. When the Jeep came to a stop, he seemed to hesitate and take his time getting out. I held my breath, thinking that he would not turn the Jeep off, but would keep going around my driveway and out of my life again, this time forever. *Why was I so afraid that he would leave? It should be more than obvious, by now, how we feel about each other now. Stop worrying!* From my vantage point, I could see him reach across to the passenger side, picking up a package. My view became blocked as he backed out and stepped away from the Jeep. When he stood up and started toward the house, I noticed the package he carried was a green paper bundle. By this time, I realized I had not moved from my spot, transfixed by his presence. He stood next to the Jeep with complete ease, shielding his eyes with his free hand and looking up into the bright, blue Arizona sky. I could tell from where I stood that he wore freshly pressed jeans, a crisp white shirt, and worn, but polished boots. His collar length hair still looked damp from his morning shower. Standing there and watching him, without him knowing it, felt as if I was watching some part of his inner being morph like the caterpillar to butterfly. His overall countenance was so serene that it made my breath catch in my throat. He turned and began walking toward the house. I shook myself back to the present, making my feet move, and was at my front door the same time the doorbell rang.

I opened the door and stood silently as he brushed past me. I could only turn and watch as the wave of heat I experienced earlier ran from my face and ended with a quiver between my legs.

"Hi," he said as he made his way into the entry and headed toward the kitchen. "I hope I'm not late."

"Hi, yourself, and no you're not late," I said, following at his heels.

"What are you doing?" I asked as he continued to walk toward the kitchen.

"Oh, these are for you, and these . . . are for your mother. Do you think she'll like them?"

When he stepped away from my marble counter top, there lay two wrapped bundles of perfect roses. He handed me the red ones. The yellow ones were a gift for my mother. He put those in the refrigerator to keep them fresh until we left.

"Oh, Joe, they're beautiful." I stood with my mouth open as he put the red ones in my arms. I cradled them like a newborn baby and bent my head to breathe in their soft, delicate scent.

"Red is for love," he told me. "I love you, Rae."

He stepped closer and looked down at me with such love and sweetness in his eyes that I thought I would not be able to find my voice.

I looked up at him startled, still transfixed by the roses. "I love you, too, Joe." I could feel my heart give a lurch as he kissed me. The roses were pressed between us as he encircled me with his strong and reassuring arms. All my past worries flew from my mind. I did indeed love him very much and wanted to be a part of his life, no matter the cost.

His face loomed inches from mine. I could smell his freshly shaved face and see the small traces of wet hair that neatly fell into place. I watched as the corners of his eyes crinkled and his mouth lifted into a slight smile. Again I felt that shiver run though me that radiated up, this time from my pelvis to my flushed face. I closed my eyes and listened to the pounding of my heart as his lips touched mine. The cold shiver I felt was replaced by his warm hands as they cupped my face and pressed my mouth to his. I no longer needed to hold the roses; they were wedged between us like a second skin. A sudden sweet fragrance was released and mixed with our own pheromones. My arms were now free to wrap around his neck, and I pressed my lips deeper into his. I never wanted to let go. *Oh, God. What was happening to me? I have lost all control.*

Joe picked me up and carried me to my bedroom. I rested my head on his chest, that familiar spot that always reassured me of his existence. I could feel his heart pounding, matching mine, thinking it would burst from my chest. I remember still clutching a few remaining roses as he laid me gently on the bed. The rest lay scattered in a scented trail down the hallway.

We watched each other as we undressed, never taking our eyes away. I ran my hands over his chest and could feel the underlying muscles jump at my touch. I bent my head and ran my tongue in circles around his hard, erect nipples. Our bodies, stretched out on the cool sheets, faced each other, touching, tasting, and inhaling as much of each other as we could, like starved flowers for the rain. I pushed him over on his back and sat lightly on his pelvis. Leaning forward, I let my upper torso, breasts, and shoulders rest on him. I nuzzled my face into his neck, smelling soap and aftershave. Using my tongue, I ran it up the outside of his neck to his ear and sucked on his earlobe. He could hear my own breath become deeper as I exhaled into his ear, while I could feel his chest rise and his breathing match mine. I slid up slightly to accommodate his growing hardness, which now was pressed between my thighs and his stomach. In one swift and effortless movement, he slid his hand over my lower back and cupped my two fleshy mounds and turned us both over so that I was now lying on my back with him pressed on top of me.

"Sweet Jesus, Joe, what are you doing?" I asked after sweeping the loose hair from my face. I watched as he now sat astride me, holding himself up on his bent knees so as not to crush me.

A devilish grin came over his face. "I just thought I would give you some of your own medicine." He bent forward and ran his tongue from my navel to my breasts, circling each one until he found his target and sucked, making me shriek with girlish-giggles.

"Oh, Joe, stop, you're tickling me. Come here and kiss me," I said, raising his face and pulling him to me. Holding his face in my hands, it was as if I could not get enough of him and I sank my mouth into his, while at the same time he slid into me. Our breaths came short and fast; sweat began to form between our chests.

I'm afraid, Joe. I am so close. I'm afraid to let go, Joe. It's okay, Rae, you're safe. Joe loves you. A burst of stars exploded in my head as the rest of my body gave off its nether spasm and I struggled for breath.

"I can't breathe. Joe, what happened? Are you okay?"

"I'm here, Rae. Everything's okay. Oh, sorry. Here, let me move off you and you might be able to catch your breath."

Joe rolled off the top of me and lay there, bathed in a sheen of sweat. I put my hand on my left breast to feel my heart thud in my chest.

The force and energy of our love that afternoon sealed our fate, like two lovers who found each other after being separated by some distant tragedy. We lay in each other's arms spent, waiting for our bodies to cool down before getting out of bed to get dressed. His eyes fluttered under closed lids while his chest heaved for breath. I watched his pulse throb in the hollow of his throat and reached to lay light fingertips against his skin, to feel his heartbeat match mine. A feeling of serenity washed over me as some inner whispering told me that we would never be apart again.

After a time, we wandered hand-in-hand to the bathroom and stood silently together under a cool shower, rinsing away our combined sweat and lovemaking juices, replacing them with the knowing revelation that ours was not to be a casual relationship.

Much later, I retraced the trail of forgotten roses, picked them up from my bedroom to the kitchen, and put their limp, water-starved stems into a crystal vase. I retrieved the yellow roses from my refrigerator and together we drove to my parent's home so they could finally meet the long-forgotten stranger who saved them and their family.

23

The Welcome

JOE OPENED THE DOOR of his Jeep for me and I settled back into the comfortable seat. He took a quiet moment before he started the ignition. I watched him as he took a deep breath and sat back to buckle his seatbelt. When he pulled out of my circular driveway and headed into town, he said, "You know, we don't have to tell your folks about us right away. They will already have a lot to think about after I meet them."

I sat across from him thinking the same thing. They were going to have a lot to absorb after they met Joe. Telling them that we had been seeing each other would be too much for them all at once.

"I think you're right. Maybe we should wait awhile before we tell them. They need to get used to the idea of you being around and someone real to them."

"Don't forget my two sisters and brother will want to meet you as well," I reminded him.

"Oh, yeah. I'm suddenly becoming quite the celebrity," Joe said with a chuckle in his voice.

"You have no idea, Joe. You have no idea," I said, looking out the Jeep window.

We rode the rest of the way in silence. I'm sure we both contemplated how the afternoon would go. There was no doubt in my mind that it would be an afternoon that none of us would soon forget.

Within the hour, we pulled up to my parents' single-story tract home in nearby Mesa. They have lived here for over thirty years, the longest they have lived anywhere. During my younger school days, we seemed to move quite a bit because of my dad's jobs, but eventually settled in Arizona.

I looked over at Joe to see if his face revealed any reluctance. He met my eyes with that relaxed, self-assured posture that immediately took away any doubts I might be feeling. He kissed me quick on my upturned lips and said, "Let's go," as he turned and grabbed the yellow roses from the backseat.

He came around my side of the Jeep to meet me, and together we walked hand in hand up the front sidewalk. My hands tingled with a nervous chill while driving up their street, but I relaxed and the chill left me as Joe's warm hand gave mine a quick squeeze.

I didn't need to ring the doorbell because just as I reached for the door, it swung open and both of my parents stood in the doorway to greet us. They must have watched from the front window that faced the street and seen us pull up into the driveway. We were greeted by the cool breeze of their air conditioning and a silent house. Their dog, Duncan, must have been sequestered away temporarily in the back bedroom. He gets overexcited by visitors and makes a general pest of himself by barking incessantly until he is convinced that the visitors are friends and not foes.

When we stepped into the front room, I felt Joe tense as I saw him turn and look around the room. I gently put my hand on his upper arm, letting him know I was still with him. I hoped this first meeting was not too much for him or my parents. I had already experienced the shock of that feeling myself and knew what it felt like to see a ghost from the past.

"Mom, Dad, I'd like you to meet a friend of mine, Joe Sullivan. He's the artist that painted *Canyon Lake*. And he's the man I told you about, the one that was with us that day at the lake. Joe, this is John and Anna Warner, my parents." I think that's what I said. The room seemed to be spinning.

"It's nice to meet you finally, Mr. and Mrs. Warner."

"Joe, it's wonderful to meet you after all these years. Please, call us John and Anna," my mother said.

"Anna, these are for you. I hope you like roses. Yellow ones were my mother's favorite. She said yellow is for joy and friendship," Joe said as he placed them in her arms.

By the flushed look on her face, my mother was clearly impressed. When she found her voice, she said, "Oh, Joe, they're beautiful. Yes, I love roses."

I stood back to watch what would happen between these three. My father quickly held out his hand to take Joe's and pulled him toward him in a quick, one-arm pat on the shoulder. My mother then embraced Joe and led him to the nearest chair, my Dad and I followed. I noticed her hasty exit to the kitchen, saying she wanted to put the roses in some water, but the tears I noticed forming in her eyes earlier threatened to run down her cheeks.

"Good Lord," my dad said, "this is unbelievable, Rae. Tell me again how you two met."

"Wait," my mother said, "before you start, let me get us all something cold to drink. I'll be right back. I have juice, iced tea, and water."

"Thanks Mom, tea would be great for me."

"Joe, what would you like?"

"I'll have tea also, thanks. Can I help you?" Joe offered.

"No, thanks. I'll just be a minute."

While we waited for Mom to return with our drinks, I told Dad that I finally found a place for Joe's painting. It now hung on my bedroom wall. Mom returned with our cold drinks and we sat quiet for a moment, and then seemed to relax and we all started talking at once.

Dad's voice broke through first, wanting to know how and when Joe came to Arizona, and, of course, how he came to be at Canyon Lake the same day as us.

Joe happily related as much about the day as he could remember and how he came to be at that perfect place in time for all of us. I took this time to sit back and watch the reaction on my parents' faces as Joe told them when he heard our screams for help. I enjoyed listening to this familiar story, told by someone else who experienced it first-hand from a different point of view. My mother's face went visibly pale as she relived those dread-filled moments when she was drowning. My dad just shook his head in amazement as he listened.

"After I pulled you all out, I didn't know what to do. The young boy's family took him quickly up shore and you two were surrounded by four suddenly quiet children who buried their faces into your wet embrace. I noticed the older girl was the only one who looked over at me as I started to back away and head toward my friends at the far end of the shoreline. I know now that it was Rae's face that looked at me. I remember her blue eyes watching me as I picked up a pair of shoes floating on the surface. She turned her face away from me, as all of you began picking up your blankets and ice chest. I started walking and by the time I turned around again, I was halfway back to my starting point and all of you were gone." Joe let out a long breath and sat back in his chair. *Now I know why Joe's eyes seemed so familiar to me when I first saw him at the ArtWalk.*

Several long moments passed before anything more was said. Both my mother and I wiped tears from our faces as we exchanged knowing glances of the truth we had just relived.

"Well . . ." my dad said as he sat back in his chair and took a deep breath. His face looked pale and his lips trembled as he struggled to gain his composure. "Joe . . . I'll be honest with you, when Rae first told us about meeting you, I had my doubts that you could really be the same man that pulled us out years ago. It just didn't seem possible, but now . . . my God, hearing you retell us the story about that day, there is no doubt in my mind that it was you."

And with that, Joe and I turned to one another with a knowing understanding that everything was going to be the way it should be from now on. The healing of that dreaded day and all the answers to our questions had finally come.

As the afternoon wore on, it became apparent that Joe experienced as much turmoil about the events as our family. He'd been haunted by nightmares for years and they only recently ceased all together since he met me and my family.

It had been an emotional afternoon for all of us as we relived the horror of that day. Mom asked us to stay for dinner, but I was more than relieved when Joe reminded me that he needed to get back to the studio and get ready for the gallery opening next week. I know that my folks were also emotionally spent from the newly discovered person in our lives and it seemed like a good time for a well-deserved break.

We stood up from our chairs and began making our way outside. Mom hugged us both and then released us, but, still holding our hands, said, "Joe, you won't be leaving us again, will you?"

"No, Anna. I think I'll be around for a while. Rae and I still have a lot to talk about," Joe said as he smiled at me, put his arm around me, and pulled me close. The warm smile on my mother's face told me all I needed to know. Joe was indeed a welcomed addition to our family.

Joe turned to open the Jeep door for me. He walked around and got in while I said my goodbyes to my mother. Dad had stood in the doorway and waved his goodbyes. I could tell that he was too emotionally caught up with the situation and wanted some distance to grasp all that he had learned today. Joe and I would have a lot to talk about in the days to come.

24

The Deception

SEVERAL WEEKS HAD PASSED since I had heard from Lee or even thought about him. So I was caught off guard when I received a message from him on my answering machine. I wondered how much, if anything, Joe had told him about us spending so much time together over the last few weeks.

"Hi, Rae, this is Lee from the gallery. I was calling to remind you about the paintings I have in the gallery that I thought you might be interested in. Please call me. I'd like to show them to you. Well . . . goodbye."

While listening to the message, his voice sounded upbeat and less stressed than the last time I had seen him. *Maybe whatever bothered him has been cleared up. I'm sure running a business can be hectic at times.* I decided to call and make an appointment to see what new pieces he had. After all, it was the least I could do, and it was because of him that I found Joe.

Two nights later, I found myself standing in front of the gallery.

Once again, it looked as though I missed him. I peered through the window and found one light glowing on his desk. I checked my watch to make sure I had the right time. When I called, Lee told me to meet him at five o'clock. I stepped away from the door and looked down the sidewalk, hoping to see him returning from an errand. I started to walk to my car for a piece of paper, wondering if I should leave a note, when I saw Lee walking toward the gallery. When he saw me, he shouted a hello.

He came hurriedly up the sidewalk, pulling out his keys as he approached the door. "Sorry Rae. I thought I would be back before you got here. Come on in," he said as he made his way toward me.

"You're not late. I just got here," I said as he ushered me into the familiar coolness of the gallery.

"Have a seat while I get things ready," he said and then disappeared into the back room. I could hear him moving around and flipping switches as lights came on in the front, illuminating the gallery in soft, white light.

I sat back in the big leather chair by his desk and glanced around at the new artwork that appeared on the wall since my last visit. I noticed a few of Joe's pieces displayed in prominent spots that would catch the eye of anyone coming into the gallery. They would be easily seen through the large store-front window. Joe was now enjoying his long awaited success in the local art community. His music was becoming more popular as well. Many therapists found it useful in their practice for the healing arts. He had told me that he was beginning to look into other ways to mass-produce it. He hired a consultant to develop a web page so his work could be available on the internet. This would provide another avenue for exposing his music and painting to more people. Lee told him that he could use the gallery as a backdrop and a place for people to come and see his work when they were in town. More patrons would soon be visiting his shop.

I again looked at my watch, wondering what was keeping Lee. I hoped that this would not take too long. I planned to meet Joe for dinner and I didn't want to keep him waiting. He made reservations at our favorite restaurant downtown overlooking the city. After everything that happened over the last few months, I was looking forward to spending a quiet, romantic dinner out with him.

Lee came back into the office area and sat down at his desk. His eyes roamed up and down me as I self-consciously crossed and re-crossed my legs.

"How have you been doing, Rae? You look great. I hope you're not planning to rush off again on me."

"Well, actually, I am meeting someone for dinner, so I can't stay too long. I just came by to see the other paintings you told me about. A friend of mine may be interested in purchasing a few for his new office building. He asked if I knew of any available artwork that would fit his needs."

"That would be great if you would pass my name along to him. I'd be happy to show him what I've got. Too bad about your having to rush off, I was hoping we could visit for a while and maybe have dinner. I guess it's my loss." He paused. "Well then, if you're short on time, we better get started." He rose from his chair and came to stand beside me, waiting for me to follow him.

I stood up and put my small evening bag under my arm.

He led me into a back room that was brightly lit, compared to the rest of the gallery. I noticed a center-island worktable that was cluttered with remnants of framing material, tools, wire, and what appeared to be miscellaneous bottles of solvents or other chemicals he used. The walls showed open shelving filled with various kinds of other supplies and materials that he used for the running of his business.

On one end, I again saw the black, metal door of the vault. It remained slightly ajar, as before. The alarm panel blinked at me with a green light as I walked past. I stood and watched Lee move to the opposite end of the workroom. I hadn't noticed until now, but a heavy tapestry with a southwest pattern stretched across the room, hung on a stout metal rod. Lee pushed it aside with his hand to reveal yet another part of the room. As I followed him, I was amazed at what I saw; a small makeshift living space, complete with a small cot, revealed itself as Lee stepped aside for me to pass.

"I sat the paintings in here so you could see them with furniture." He must have sensed my hesitation upon entering his private quarters because he said, "Oh, I just use this on occasion when I'm working late and don't want to drive home. Come on in."

"It's nice that you have the space for this. I can see where it might come in handy sometimes, especially after the evening ArtWalks." I walked toward the pictures hung on the wall and started to browse, looking at the various landscapes.

"While you're looking at the paintings, how would you like some tea? It will take me just a minute."

"Thanks, that sounds good. If you're sure you have the time."

"Oh, I have the time," I heard Lee say over his shoulder.

Behind me, I could hear Lee in the small kitchen area that housed a microwave and countertop refrigerator. While moving from one painting to another, I heard Lee run water from the sink into a pot and then the microwave start to hum.

The art was very interesting and something I thought my friend would, in fact, be interested in for his new office space. The paintings expressed subtle Southwest undertones, yet had a very modern feel to them. I made a mental note to call my friend, Sam, in the morning and suggest that he come down himself to take a look.

My concentration on the art must have been broken because I could no longer hear Lee in the background. I felt a sudden presence behind me and a slight lift to the hairs on the back of my neck. I turned around startled to find Lee directly in back of me.

"Well, what you do think of these paintings? Is it something your friend might be interested in?"

I could feel his breath stir the loose hairs and tickle the back of my neck. I took a step sideways, out of his direct path and uttered, "Huh, yes. I think he might be interested. I'll give him a call tomorrow and suggest that he call you for an appointment."

I could smell beer on his breath as he leaned into me. I didn't dodge quickly enough, and his lips brushed the side of my face. I put my arms up to his chest to push him away, and I felt sudden pressure as he grabbed both my wrists in one hand and held me there.

"Lee, what are you doing? Let me *go!*" I said, trying to keep the panic down in my voice. "Why are you doing this?" I looked up, stunned, into a flushed red face and penetrating eyes that made my knees begin to shake.

He laughed as he said, "*Why?* You ask me why? I've wanted you, Rae, ever since that first time I saw you. You've done everything to avoid me. I can be good for you, Rae, even better than Joe." His lips curled in a devilish grin.

"What's Joe got to do with this? Lee, *let me go!* You're hurting my wrists." I continued to pull against his hands, but they felt like iron cuffs around my wrists.

"I'm never going to let you go. You're not going to get away from me this time," he said, almost breathless. He dragged me over to the workbench. My feet stumbled over one another as I tried to regain my balance. My evening bag had fallen free from under my arm and lay somewhere behind me. *If I could get it, I could use my cell phone. Oh my God. Joe doesn't know where I am!*

I struggled to twist out of his grip, but he only tightened his hands around my wrists. I looked down at the workbench and saw several pieces of duct tape precut and stuck to the edge of the table. I hadn't noticed them earlier. I started desperately trying to get away by kicking and twisting my body against his. Using one hand, he took one piece of tape and wrapped it tightly around my wrists.

"Oh, Rae, come on baby, don't fight me. I don't want to get rough with you. Or, maybe you like it rough?" He bent his head again to kiss me, but I saw it coming and turned away quickly to avoid his thick, wet lips. His slap, instead, came at the side of my head, temporarily stunning me. I remained on my feet as tears stung my eyes and I fought to clear them.

He pulled me to the nearest chair and pushed me into it. He used another piece of tape to wrap around my ankles. I could smell his sweat and stale beer as he knelt in front of me. I had to take several deep breaths and swallow hard to keep the bile from forming in my throat.

"Lee, you bastard, *let me go!*" I screamed at him. "Joe will find me and then he will kill you." I struggled against the tape, but it didn't do any good. It only twisted tighter into my skin. My mind swirled. *Think Rae! Think!*

"Now, Rae. What kind of talk is that? You've surprised me. You're one little hellcat. I think we're going to get along together just fine in Europe. We can keep each other warm." I looked up at him again, bewildered. *Europe? What the hell is he talking about?* He slapped the last piece of tape over my mouth before I could tell him what I would like to with his balls.

"You don't know this, but I had to leave Colorado once before because of that bitch ex-wife of mine. I've taken care of that now too, so it will be just you and me," he said as he continued to wrap duct tape around my ankles and wrists. My breath came faster, puffing through my nose. I could feel the sweat begin to trickle under my arms and down between my breasts.

I continued to twist and struggle from his grasp as he picked me up and carried me into the vault. *Oh, God,*

I thought. *This can't be happening, not now. Not when I've just found Joe. I can't lose him.* That was the last thing I remembered before Lee put a nasty smelling rag over my nose, and the room faded to black around me.

"I am sorry, Rae. I didn't want to have to do it this way. I thought you would be more willing to play along with me, but . . . Oh, well. You'll come around to my way of thinking soon enough. Once we're in Europe, you'll forget all about Joe. We'll live in style. You'll have everything you want. Just wait, Rae, you'll see. I keep my promises," Lee said as he took her down to the vault and laid her gently on the blanket he prepared for her behind his cache of canvases. He didn't want her to wake up too soon. He still needed to move several trunks to the SUV before he propped her into the seat next to him. His plane to the East Coast wouldn't be leaving until midnight, and he wanted to make sure she would be awake for the red-eye out of Phoenix. He made his way up the steps from the vault with a satisfying smirk on his face.

25

The Dinner

JOE PACED IN THE front lobby of the restaurant. He looked at his watch. *It is after six o'clock, where is she? I knew I should have picked her up, but she said she had an errand to do and would meet me here. Calm down,* he told himself, *She's just running late. But she's never late.* Joe ran his hand through his hair as a nervous gesture and made a second pass through the front entrance, hoping to see her car pull into the parking lot.

Joe had been planning this night for weeks. Over the last few months, he and Rae spent so much time together that he knew he never wanted to be apart from her. He finally made his decision to ask her to marry him. *My life has changed so much since I met her. I would have never been able to put my guilt to rest over my stepfather or understood the reason why I was there to help her parents. It all fits. We fit.*

"Damn it! where is she? Why hasn't she called me?" he said, a little too loudly. A passing couple turned to look back at him as they entered the restaurant. He checked his cell phone again for the umpteenth time to make sure it was on and that his battery was fully charged as he continued to pace.

Joe called her house from his cell phone, but only got her answering machine. Now, looking at his watch again, it was seven o'clock. He went back into the restaurant and canceled his reservation. He walked, half ran to the parking lot, and got in his Jeep and headed for her house. *God forbid she's sick or had an accident.*

Driving faster than he normally would, he reached her house to find the outside security lights on and a lit pathway up the driveway. He threw the Jeep in park and barely stopped it in time, getting out amid a flurry of dust and gravel. He ran to the front of the house and used the key she had given him weeks ago. They exchanged keys so that they could come and go freely between their two homes. He disabled the alarm and started through the house. Calling out as he went, he gasped for breath, while his heart pounded in his chest. "Rae, are you home. Honey, where are you?"

Dashing from room to room, he noticed nothing appeared to be disturbed and he could find Rae nowhere. Standing in the middle of her bedroom, he could see the remnants of her getting ready for their planned dinner. The closet door stood open to reveal scattered shoes and her workout clothes lying on the floor. He closed his eyes and sniffed the air, his heart resuming its normal beat, and tried to focus, to gather his thoughts. He could smell traces of her perfume and the remnants of the candles she likes to light as she dressed. When he opened his eyes, he continued to scan the room for some indication of where she might have gone. The red roses he had given her were now stiff and dry as they stood in an empty crystal vase on her bedside table. His eyes caught the red light flashing on her answering machine. He hesitated for a moment, wondering if he should listen to the messages. *What the hell . . . she can be pissed with me later for invading her privacy.*

The first message was from her mother, Anna, asking how she was and to call her when she had time. The next message sent sharp prickles of tension up his neck at the familiar voice coming from the machine. Joe sat on the edge of the bed with his hands on his legs for support and leaned forward to listen as Lee's voice said, "Hello Rae, just calling to remind you about our appointment tonight. I'm looking forward to showing you the paintings I have saved for you. Don't forget, five o'clock."

Joe sat, frozen in place as he realized where Rae had gone. *That must have been the errand she told me about before meeting me for dinner. Oh, Rae.* He thought. *What have you done? Lee, you son-of-a-bitch, if you hurt her, I swear . . .* Joe didn't finish the sentence because he was already out the door and heading toward the Jeep.

26

The Discovery

WHILE JOE DROVE TOWARD the gallery, his thoughts dwelled only on Rae. *Please let her be all right. Dear God in heaven, don't let me lose her again.*

The traffic was heavy on this typical Friday night in downtown Scottsdale. It looked like the usual party crowd was out and filling the streets. Joe zigzagged in and out of the traffic, trying to make all the green lights. When he finally pulled up in front of the gallery, the side street was quiet and only a few couples strolled along, looking in windows. Joe got out of the Jeep and stood quietly for a moment, listening for any sounds coming from inside. He, too, peered in the window and saw only the one desk lamp on. A few other spotlights glowed in the black darkness from within, casting eerie shadows on the wall.

From his vantage point, craning his neck at an angle, he could see the alarm panel on the opposite wall. The light blinked green. *That's odd*, he thought. *It should be red when it's armed. Lee must still be here.*

Joe walked around to the back of the gallery to check Lee's parking space. When he turned the corner to the back entrance, his way was illuminated by a few wide-ly-spaced streetlights. He found Lee's designated park-ing spot, but his SUV was not parked there. He stood, trying to slow his breathing, while his eyes continued to adjust to the semi-darkness. He spotted Lee's SUV parked close to the back entrance of the gallery, as if he were unloading supplies.

Joe approached the vehicle with trepidation. Placing his hand on the hood, he noticed that it was still warm. He walked to the driver's side window and saw that the keys were on the front seat. *He must be coming back here soon if he left his keys laying here.* The door was unlocked so he quickly opened the door and grabbed the keys and put them in his pocket. *If I'm wrong about all this, I'll explain to Lee that I'm crazy. But if I'm not, I want to try and slow him down as much as possible. Whatever his intentions, I want some answers before he leaves.* He closed the door to the SUV softly, so as to not draw any unwarranted at-tention, and walked to the back entrance of the gallery.

The entrance on this side of the building was a smooth-fitting metal door that had only a lip-like pull handle. He used his hands to feel the door for the han-dle and gave a slight pull of pressure. It opened lightly in his hand. *This door is never left unlocked; he must be moving things in and out of here. But why would he be doing it at this time of night?* Joe wondered as he cautiously en-tered the back of Lee's gallery. The only lights that were on in the workroom were the automatic security lights. He could see dim illumination coming from the front of the gallery as he made his way through the work-room. Walking slowing in unfamiliar surroundings, he could smell cleaning solvents and a slight trace of the nauseating smell he recognized as ether. They both had used these solvents in their work with paints. Once his eyes adjusted to the darkness, there was enough light for him to see that several things that would normally be on the workbench now lay scattered on the floor. He continued to look around the room and noticed an overturned chair. He bent to upright it and a slight reflection of light caught his eye. He stooped down to find a shiny, metal object and picked it up. He stood up and went to where the light was better and found in his hand a silver and turquoise dragonfly pin. His heart gave a lurch when recognition came. It was one of Rae's favorite pieces of jewelry. He had seen her wear it many times. The clasp had a slight bend to it, as though it had been ripped from the wearer. He closed his hand over the pin and put it in his front shirt pocket. Walking cautiously now, he continued to make his way around the workroom. At one end he found himself in front of a curtain of some sort and stopped himself from hastily pushing it aside. He hesitated long enough to listen for any sound or motion that may be behind it. Hearing none, he raised his hand and pushed it gently across the open space. Another small light on a far counter showed him that no one was there. He could make out a chair and a small cot, along with framed artwork hanging on the walls. He started to turn when his eyes again caught a smaller, dark object lying on the floor. He knelt down to take a closer look and picked up a woman's handbag. He opened it quickly to find Rae's wallet and car keys. Her cell phone glowed green in his hand as he took it out, making sure it was on vibrate, and slipped it into his jacket pocket. He laid her handbag on the workroom table.

Now, he knew. Rae was here, but where? He stood still to listen, but so far all he could hear was his ragged breath and the thudding of his heart, along with the hum of the air conditioning. From behind him came a faint glow of light. He turned around and quickly crouched behind the workbench. As he did so, a large door opened up from the back of the room and Joe saw Lee's bulk emerge from steps that lead to the basement-level vault. The door remained open as Lee walked to the workbench and, with a toss of his arm, he threw something on the table and it landed with a soft thud. Joe remained where he was, listening for any sound of Rae, but heard nothing. Lee moved around the room, picking up things from the table and cabinets. He mumbled something Joe couldn't make out, only hearing an occasional curse.

From where he crouched, Joe looked for something or some way to knock Lee off his guard. He needed to get to Rae. *Why was Lee doing this? Rae's initial feelings about Lee had been right. She sensed something was wrong. I had no reason to suspect Lee of any wrong doing in my dealings with him. Damn, why didn't I follow through on Rae's intuition?* He ran his hands under the raised base of the workbench, hoping to find something he could use against Lee. He couldn't risk using the cell phone right now. His hand touched a long, metal pipe that lay forgotten, covered in a light layer of dust, under the cabinet. He curled his fingers around it and drew it to him as quietly as he could.

Lee continued to move around the workroom. He

walked to his desk without suspecting someone was watching him and gathered what he needed for his hasty exit from Arizona. He would come back for the paintings later, he took only what he could now. He had Rae quietly bound down in the vault until he was ready to move her to his SUV waiting out back.

When Lee walked into the workroom from the front of the gallery, he brushed against the workroom table. Looking down, he recognized something familiar, but strangely out of place. Taking a step back, he picked up Rae's handbag. *I don't remember seeing Rae put that here.* His brain raced ahead. He remembered grabbing her wrists as he pulled her out of the chair. It must have fallen from her grasp then, but on the floor, not here. His eye caught a slight movement, but his brain didn't register the action until it was too late. The darkened figure moved quickly and struck him a savage blow to the knees. His kneecaps exploded with pain as he fell to the floor where he stood.

"Arghhh, you son-of-a-bitch."

He rolled over on his back to see Joe Sullivan standing over him. Why didn't that surprise him? He hoped Joe would not have tried to interfere, but somehow he knew he would have to deal with him, too. He tried to sit up, but the movement shot pain to his brain. Before he could move again, Joe landed on him and shoved his knees to his chest, pushing the last of his breath out of his lungs. He held the metal pipe across his throat, pressing firmly to hold him in a prone position.

"Lee, I don't care if you steal this whole damn gallery. Tell me where Rae is or, so help me God, this will be your last breath!" Joe shook with rage and struggled for his own breath. He pushed the metal pipe tighter against Lee's throat. Joe could hear Lee fight for air and he released his grip just enough to hear him say, "Vault." Then Lee passed out.

Joe sat back on his heels and threw the pipe to the ground and raced toward the narrow space of the vault, swinging the heavy, metal door open. Joe tore down the stairs, fighting against the bright light of the basement, trying to focus his eyes. He quickly scanned the floor and walls for any signs of Rae.

"Rae, where are you?" His shouts went unanswered. The vault housed stacks of bronze statues, unframed canvases, and black, silver jewelry cases laid open all around the room. He pushed aside boxes and crates, calling her name. He heard no response.

He stopped and stood still in the middle of the room. *She has to be here,* he kept saying to himself. His eyes fell on several large, framed landscapes he recognized at once. They were the ones he completed for his commissioned work that Lee was holding for him until the buyer was ready. He ran to them and moved them aside. There, behind his paintings, was Rae. She lay with her back against the wall, her hair covering her face. His hands ran over her inert frame, quickly searching for obvious blood or broken bones. He found none, but her hands, feet, and mouth were taped. He could tell, by the thin spirals of duct tape, that she must have struggled against the bindings because her wrists were ringed raw. He moved her carefully to the center of the room. His hand went immediately to her neck to feel for her pulse. He whispered a prayer of thanks when he felt a faint heartbeat. He peeled away the piece from across her mouth as carefully as possible for fear of taking skin with it. He gently rubbed her face and called her name, trying to rouse her. He could see a slight flutter of her eyes behind closed lids as she took a deep breath.

"Rae, Rae. Wake up. It's me, Joe. You're safe now." At the sound of his voice, she came full awake and moaned.

When her eyes regained their focus, she looked up into Joe's forlorn face. His eyes were gleaming wet and his breathing was a little ragged. "Oh, Joe!" she whimpered. She buried her face into his shoulder and they sat huddled together on the cold floor in the semi-darkness of the vault.

Rae remained on the floor with Joe's coat over her shoulders. He left to go to the workroom to find something to cut the tape from her feet and wrists. She sat shivering, taking a deep breath, and felt weak with relief.

Joe came back downstairs with scissors and his cell phone.

"Joe, what about Lee? Where is he?"

Joe sat beside Rae, cutting through the duct tape.

"You don't have to worry about him. I used some of this stuff on him," he said, holding up remnants of tape. "I also called the police. They'll be here soon." When he freed her of the sticky binding, he helped her to her feet, and they stood together, holding each other in the center of the room until they heard sirens. Slowly, arm-in-arm, they made their way up the stairs and out of the vault.

27

The Beginning

THE EVENTS OF THE last week left Joe and Rae emotionally drained. Joe had difficulty coming to terms with the fact that his friend and business associate was a wanted man. He soon found out that Lee Beck had been living a lie for quite some time.

During the investigation, the police told him that Lee Beck, aka Ben Andrews, had been arrested for assaulting his ex-wife in Colorado. She disappeared soon after the divorce and has not been found. Lee jumped bail and left the state. He had been under surveillance by the police for suspicion of being involved in an art theft ring in the Southwest. They found enough evidence in the gallery to put him away for a long time. Once the investigation was over, Joe would be able to recover his paintings. His artwork, as well as everything else in the gallery, was considered evidence and could not be released until after Lee's trial. Because of Joe and Rae's involvement with Lee, they were both summoned to give their testimony at Lee's trial. The trial made front-page news in all the local papers. A scandal of this magnitude in the art world had been almost too much for Rae and Joe to deal with.

After many months of court appearances and dodging newspaper reporters, Rae looked forward to spending more time alone with Joe and her family. Needless to say, they were quite shaken up by Lee's intent to kidnap Rae and take her with him to Europe to sell the stolen pieces of art. She was very thankful that Joe was there, once again, in her time of need.

They were relaxing together on the patio of his studio the following Sunday morning. It rained the night before and the ground was still damp with moisture. The early morning mist had not evaporated, and the air was scented with desert citrus and creosote.

Joe sat strumming his guitar, trying to work out a new melody. Rae was leisurely stretched out on a chaise lounge, listening to the subtle cords of music as he played.

"You know, I've been thinking," Rae said as she gathered her legs under her and sat up, looking again at those wonderful hands of his.

Joe stopped playing and looked at Rae. *God, she's beautiful,* he thought as he put his guitar down and moved to sit in front of her.

"What have you been thinking?" he said, and looked into her smiling face.

"I've been thinking that we should move in together. We spend so much time together, and it would save us from having to drive back and forth. What do you think?" Rae looked into Joe's face and kissed him.

"Is that the only reason we should move in together, to save on gas?" he grinned.

"Joe, no, of course not, you know what I mean." Teasingly, she pushed him away.

Laughing, Joe got up and sat beside her now. "Come here, I want to ask you something." He put one arm around her and drew her close.

Rae moved in closer and kissed his neck. She could smell the lingering remnants of their sex from the night before on him and was reminded of it as a quiver passed across her pelvis. She inhaled deeply and looked into his face.

"Do you remember the night we planned to have dinner together in Phoenix? The night you didn't show up?" he looked into her eyes for a glimmer of recognition. They hadn't talked much about that night since it happened. Rae always seemed on the verge of flight or fight, so he hadn't wanted to talk about it until she was ready. He wasn't sure if now was the time either, and hoped it would not panic her. He felt her shudder as if to throw off some bad vibe. He continued to sit close to her and hold her.

"Yes, Joe. I remember. I still can't believe what that madman did."

"I know. I can't either. But do you remember the special evening we had planned?" he said as he kissed her softly. "Oh, Rae, I was so scared that night. I thought I lost you again. I don't ever want to lose you. I want to spend the rest of my life with you." He pulled her to him and held the back of her head with his hand. "Rae, I love you. Forever will never be long enough for me to love you."

She pulled away from him and looked at his face. Those steel-blue eyes and dark lashes searched her face.

"Rae, I love you. Will you marry me?" he said slowly, looking directly into her eyes so that there would be no misunderstanding.

⁓₩₩⁓

I sat stunned for a moment and felt myself being lifted to my feet. He stepped closer and looked down at me with such love and tenderness in his eyes I thought I would not be able to speak.

"Well . . . Will you?" His mesmerizing smile overtook his face.

"Yes." I finally found my voice. Tears spilled down my face. He kissed me on the lips, and then covered my face, neck, and ears with his lips as if not knowing what to kiss first.

⁓₩₩⁓

I could feel her body rise as I kissed her. Then, I heard her say "yes" again with a sigh.

EPILOGUE

A ND SO . . .

When all such manner of things came together in my life, I was able to tell this story. Please know that these two people, Rae Warner and Joe Sullivan, came to a happy ending. They didn't know it, but they had been looking for each other their whole lives. It wasn't until events folded on top of one another that they were able to come together according to their own time and place. This was my story told through their lives. Thank you for letting me share it with you.

Melanie Gaines
2006

ABOUT THE AUTHOR

MELANIE GAINES LIVES IN the Sonoran Desert of Arizona, southwest of Canyon Lake. She earned her Bachelor of Arts in Education from Arizona State University and a Master of Arts in Education from Northern Arizona University. She has worked as an elementary school teacher, library/media specialist, and a reading specialist. She is working on three children's picture books, short stories, and prose. *Canyon Lake* is her first novel.

Printed in the United States
66125LVS00002B/21